On Shallowed Ground

including
Dr Barker's Scientific Metamorphical Prostate Health Formula®
and Other Stories, Poems, Comedy and Dark Matter
from the Center of the Universe

By Walt Pilcher

Foreword by Samuel L Clemens

On Shallowed Ground

including
Dr Barker's Scientific Metamorphical Prostate Health Formula®
and Other Stories, Poems, Comedy and Dark Matter
from the Center of the Universe

By Walt Pilcher

Foreword by Samuel L Clemens

FIRST EDITION

Published by Fantastic Books Publishing
ISBN (eBook) 978-1-909163-84-3
ISBN (Print) 978-1-909163-85-0

Praise for On Shallowed Ground

You'd have to go to the Bible for such a brilliant collection of stories of international intrigue, domestic crises, incredible ironies, history, the triumph of good over evil, comedy, satire, and tender romance (yes, even sex) as is found here in *On Shallowed Ground* ... or to the library.

Bupkis Reviews

Walt Pilcher writes in a style unhampered by the inconvenient presumption that anyone may be reading the book.

Book City Reviews

There is a bright and successful career ahead for Walt Pilcher, perhaps even as a writer.

Durango Falcone

Written with the pen of a master storyteller, which Mr Pilcher purchased on eBay from the estate of a famous author.

Winnovation Magazine

A bright and witty book worth reading? I couldn't ... put it down. Now.

The Surgeon General

Reports of my death have been greatly exaggerated.

Mark Twain

In this brilliant collection of stories of international intrigue, domestic crises, incredible ironies, history, the triumph of good over evil, comedy, satire, and tender romance (yes, even sex), the reader is spared the clichés so often rampant in a mass market book. Mr Pilcher has saved them all for the dust jacket notes.

Durango Falcone

What page is the sex on?

Victoria County School Board

Contents

Dedication

First, to three of my venerable teachers at Washington-Lee High School in Arlington, VA, all now deceased (which I swear I had nothing to do with): Mrs Miller Vice (yes, Vice) in English turned me on to the genius of James Thurber, Robert Benchley and Mark Twain when she perceived I had a penchant for satire and parody if not for punctuation. Luckily, I already knew of Stan Freburg, Bob & Ray and *Mad Magazine*. Miss Jane Elliott in History brought that subject to life while saving me from a too-late discovery that history stores probably weren't going to be hiring when I graduated. Mr Stanley Book (yes, Book) taught Government and as our Class Advisor was always ready to give advice (hence Advisor), to defend us from the Administration when we occasionally transgressed a school rule, and to participate in such transgressions when he thought it might be fun.

Then also to Mr Science (not his real name), a teacher at Williamsburg Jr. High who one day, after asking us to turn a large, full wooden bookcase to the wall, chucked an authentic 6' African spear into the back of it, tearing it asunder and shredding many books (yes, books). All to demonstrate ... what, exactly? I don't know, but I can tell you I never turned my back on Mr Science again until I graduated. For me the lesson was, You Can't Make This Stuff Up, a condition of our fallen world that has informed my writing ever since.

In addition, to my two fellow student partners in parody, Lt Colonel Henry J "Rocky" Colavita (US Army, Ret) and the late John

N McCune, Esq, who together with me when we weren't doing sketch comedy on my Wilcox-Gay tape recorder or in McCune's case waxing the front bench seat of his Studebaker Commander so his dates would helplessly slide over against him whenever he made a right turn (this was before seat belts), established the true length of Chain Bridge across the Potomac River in Washington DC as 3,872 BTS, the BTS being our standard unit of measure, the Bathroom Tissue Square.

Finally, to John G Sommer (yes, Sommer), my colleague on WESU-FM at Wesleyan University in Middletown, CT, now living in Dummerston, VT (yes, Dummerston). Our weekly radio show, aptly named "To Be Announced" because we rarely took time to prepare anything before air time (due to being serious about our studies and all), featured original sketch comedy and phony interviews mingled with rousing selections of British marching music. This was long before Monty Python, who obviously got the idea from us. Highlights included our resident futurist and prognosticator, Gerard Sandflea (yes, Sandflea), who in one memorable interview gave us three rock solid, and different, dates for the End of the World, all of which have long since passed, unless I've missed something, and John's incisive coverage of my re-creation of a lunar eclipse right in the studio.

Other teachers contributed importantly to my literary development, but sadly I have forgotten who they were. No doubt upon hearing of this, John G Sommer will say I have lost my faculties.

Like I said, you can't make this stuff up.

Foreword

I only knew Walt Pilcher about five minutes before he invited me into his man cave and showed me his collection of margarita recipes from around the world. "Someday I'm going to write a book about these," he said. "I'm going to call it *Margarita Recipes from Around the World*. It will have pictures and everything."

It's a big collection. Some are on three-by-five cards, some torn out of magazines, some scribbled on paper napkins, and a lot of them are on rough scraps of paper with peculiar looking stains. All have dates and the names of restaurants, towns and countries from as far away as Canada.

"Have you ever been to any of these places?" I asked.

"You mean besides La Tarjeta Verde Mexican Restaurant up the street here?"

"Well ... yeah, I guess."

"Of course not," Walt answered, sounding a little irritated. "Although I did have lunch in Tijuana once. But I forgot to order a margarita. Anyhow, I can get what I need from the Internet."

As far as I know Walt hasn't written that book yet. But he did write this one, which I've promised to read as soon as I have time. He assures me it's very good and that I will enjoy it. He says it has lots of interesting stuff in it, like funny stories and poems and things, but not the sappy kind of poems I don't like. I believe him. He's never lied to me before, so there is no reason to think he would start now. That's why I can honestly recommend this book to you. And I've known most of you even less than five minutes. Apparently, that is how things work in this modern age of the Internet and electronical relationships and experiences, at least according to my son Mark and my grandchildren, who have also promised to read this book when they have time, probably on their iPhones between texting and Tweeties or whatever they call it.

I was as surprised as anyone when Walt asked me to write this Foreword. I'm happy to do it because he is probably going to turn out to be a good customer. However, I think he is mistaking me for some famous writer or other. I don't know why, but it wouldn't be the first time.

Really I only came to fix his toilet.

Samuel L Clemens

Clemens & Sons Plumbing, Inc.

Serving the Triad Area since 1986

Call (336) 555-3345 Day or Night

www.csplumbers.com

"Flushing your pain right down the drain!"

Introduction

Did anyone ever say to you, "Hey (your name), you should write a book!"

Certainly nobody ever said that to me. On the other hand, I'll bet nobody ever said, "Hey, you shouldn't write a book!" either. Right? So at least we have that in common for starters, and I can tell we're warming up to each other already. You're going to like this book. Which I wrote because nobody told me not to.

It seems to me that should be enough of an introduction, but I've noticed most book introductions are quite a bit longer, so I guess if I want this to look like a real book, I should add some more.

Now that I've established why I wrote it, or at least why I didn't not write it, maybe I should tell you what it's about.

It is a dark and stormy book.

It's not a novel, so therefore it's not about any one thing. However, it could be there's a common theme running throughout, like for example, the influence of left handed cross-eyed French impressionists on modern art. Or global warming. Or (wait for it) ... love. While it's certainly true not much has been written about the influence of left handed cross-eyed French impressionists on global warming, or love, this isn't the book to rectify that lack. There are probably other books that do that. No, there is no particular theme here. There may be a common thread or two within some sections, as you will see, but otherwise it's not intended to be tied together particularly well at all.

Nor need it be. It's a wandering minstrel, this book. It's an eclectic (look it up) collection of short stories and fictional non-fiction pieces with poems and songs salted throughout. Most are recent but a couple of them go back to the 1970's. I've updated the language in those because no one had heard of the Internet, smartphones, or a mouse you keep on your desk back then.

To those of you saying, Wow, it took this guy 40 years to write a book, I say, Okay, and how long did it take Moses? Forty years in the wilderness and he's a perennial bestseller. Quality takes time.

Get ready for the doting father who has himself declared dead. Fall in love with the banker turned baker who finds a new recipe for herself. Enjoy a literally lighthearted look at prostates. Get a new take, so to speak, on alien abduction. Chose a religion. Predict your future by remembering the past. Learn where you and everybody else really live. Speaking of recipes, make a whole bunch of cookies or a tremendous amount of soup using official, but colloquial, government weights and measures. Avoid artichokes. Expect silver bullets, stampeding gazeboes, spontaneous combustion, and so much more.

There's even an interactive story where *you* get to choose the ending.

A few of these pieces have been published elsewhere, and attribution is given as appropriate. The others are either moldering in some editor's slush pile or have contributed to my collection of rejection slips which, before the age of e-mail, threatened to swamp my small office here in the basement of the North Carolina home that I share with my wife, Carol, an artist and long-suffering reader and critiquer of my work. She's not so sure about some of the material in this book, by the way.

And also by the way, nobody ever said to me, "Hey (my name), you should get all your stuff together into a book." I thought of that all by myself.

"But what about that title, *On Shallowed Ground?*"

Oh yeah? What about it? Hey (your name), write your own book and call it whatever you want. This one is mine. (But at least now someone has told you you should write a book.)

And further also by the way, about (my name). You know me as Walt Pilcher, but I'll bet you've never heard of me. Maybe I'm actually someone else, perhaps a famous bestselling author like Stephen King, Orson Scott Card, JK Rowling, O Henry, Stephen Fry, Mark Twain, or Durango Falcone, writing under an alias, a pseudonym, a pen name, or a *nom de plume*, or maybe all four, because I don't want to confuse my usual readers. Or maybe I'm not just one person but two or three of us who've decided to get together and have some fun at your expense. Maybe we're famous. Maybe not. Google me all you want; you'll still never know for sure. And when "Walt Pilcher" becomes a famous bestselling author and wants to write something different, he too will change his name so as not to confuse his usual readers.

In any case, read on. You'll laugh. You'll cry. You'll wonder why. These stories and poems will make you glad you weren't absent from school the day they taught reading.

Walt Pilcher
Greensboro, NC USA
November 2015

Prologue
On Shallowed Ground:
The Real Story of Moses and the Burning Bush

Here comes 80 year old Moses, taking a break from writing the Old Testament. He's walking in the far side of the desert with a flock of his father-in-law's sheep as is his habit of an afternoon, there being no senior center where he can go play a couple hands of bridge once in a while with the few friends he has left among the Israelites after the little murder incident 40 years ago. Or maybe learn that new mahjong game somebody brought back from the East.

"They never forgive; they never forget," he frequently thinks. "Truly they are a stiff-necked people. Me, all alone out here in this wasteland, putting together a history book probably no one will ever read and talking to sheep. And they never write. My old friends, I mean, not the sheep. Except my brother, Aaron, but that's only when he wants something."

By now he's getting close to Mt. Horeb, known by all as The Mountain of God, although if any of the mountains didn't belong to God, he didn't know which ones they were. All of a sudden, he sees flames coming out of a bush, but the bush is not burning up. So Moses thinks, "I will go over and see this strange sight—why the bush does not burn up."

When he goes over to look, God calls to him from within the bush, "Moses! Moses!"

And Moses says, "Whoa!! What the …??" while he's thinking, "Apparently they don't call this the far side for nothing!"

"Is that you, God? Uh … maybe I'll take off my sandals, okay? See, I'm taking off my sandals here."

"Do not come any closer," God says, "and keep your sandals on. You think I am going to let you stand on holy ground after what you did? You should live so long. Just stay over there in that slight depression by the road, which I will call the 'shallowed ground,' while we have a little talk."

So Moses thinks, "See, even God hates me." Grumpily, he puts his sandals back on.

Then God says, "I am the God of your father, the God of Abraham, the God of Isaac and the God of Jacob."

At this, Moses hides his face, because he is afraid to look at God.

"Hey, look at me when I am talking to you!"

"But won't I die if I see you?"

"Who told you that? Where do you stiff-necked people get these ideas?"

"But …"

"Besides, do you think I really look like a stupid burning bush?"

"Well …"

"Just listen for a minute," says God. "I have indeed seen the misery of My people. I have heard them crying out, and I am concerned about their suffering. And now, yes, the cry of the Israelites has reached me. So I have come down to rescue them and to bring them up into a good and spacious land, a land flowing with milk and honey, and mostly to make them feel a lot better about themselves. Do you, Moses, know what their problem is?"

"Well …"

"*I* know what their problem is!"

"Well, You would, wouldn't You?"

"Do not get smart! Do you know what it is?"

"Well …"

"I will tell you what it is. My people take themselves too seriously, that is what it is!"

"Okay …"

"So now, go. I am sending you with a message to My people, to bring My people up out of their depression and misery. To bring them joy!"

But Moses says to God, "Who am I that I should go and bring joy to the Israelites? I'm as miserable as they are. More, even. But the milk and honey bit sounds good."

"And that is only part of the package," says God. "There is also love, peace, patience, kindness, goodness, faithfulness, gentleness and self-control, the latter being something I know you, especially, can use."

"I like it. How'd You come up with that list, anyway?"

"Let us just say I have a way with Words. You would understand if I let you live long enough to write the New Testament too."

"Right, I should live so long."

"I call that list 'the fruit of the Spirit.'"

"Fruit? WhaddaYa mean, fruit? Didn't we already get in enough trouble with fruit back there with Adam and Eve? Enough with the fruit already!"

"That was an apple, Moses. You cannot compare apples and … uh … other fruit, if you know what I mean. I am talking figurative fruit."

"Excuse me, but maybe all this talking figuratively is going to cause some confusion. You know, down the road, so to speak."

"Never mind that now. The point is, I want My people to quit worrying and be happy. They should relax. I am their God, after all, and I am on their side."

"Okay, here I am. But you know I'm unaccustomed to public speaking."

"Then I will let your brother, Aaron, help you. He has got a mouth on him, that boy."

"Still, if the people don't like what I say, they'll stone me," protests Moses.

"Oy! You people and your stoning! No doubt that is how you got such stiff necks, from stoning all the time! They will not stone you!"

If you've ever been to Israel, you were undoubtedly struck, so to speak, by how the landscape is strewn with rocks and stones of all sizes and shapes. They are everywhere, like massive ancient hailstones that never melted. In the apparent absence of many other sports in Bible times, it's no wonder the Israelites took to throwing rocks at each other whenever they got mad, which was often. To this day, there are very few glass houses in Israel.

Moses says to God, "Okay, suppose I go to the Israelites and say to them, 'The God of your fathers has sent me to you,' and they ask me, 'What is his name?' Then what shall I tell them?"

And God says to Moses, "I AM WHO I AM. This is what you are to say to the Israelites: 'I AM has sent me to you.' Now stop rolling your eyes. You think just because I AM in a burning bush I cannot see you smirking over there? Go, assemble the elders of Israel and say to them, 'The LORD, the God of your fathers—the God of Abraham, Isaac and Jacob—appeared to me and said: I have watched over you, and I have promised to bring you up out of your misery. So now I command you with this, which shall be known as the 11th Commandment …'"

"Wait! There are 10 other Commandments already?"

"Um, we will get to that. All in good time. But for now, I command you with this, which down the road shall be known as the 11th Commandment: Stop worrying, relax, have fun, eat, drink, play music, play golf, sing, dance, wear jewelry, grow beards, enjoy yourselves! Except for pork, of course. On that one I am firm."

22

"That's it? That's Your message?"

"You've got it," says God. "Basically, I want you to tell My people to let themselves go!"

And that is the spirit of this book. Freedom! Enjoy yourself. And remember, you heard it from Moses, not me.

Stories & Poems You'll Wish You'd Written

Eat your hearts out, O Henry & Robert Frost

Life After

(Originally published in *Fresh Magazine*, October 2012)

She jumped, startled.

"I'm not here," he said, with a tiny smirk.

"Oh, right. I forgot," snorted Julie, his middle child, all grown up now.

He was skulking through the house in sneakers, and she didn't hear him climbing the drop-down stairs to the attic where she was going through his old collections of this and that, grumbling as she worked. It was hot up there, and he didn't plan on staying long.

"How on earth am I supposed to decide what to do with all this ... this stuff? Sixty-eight years' worth of *stuff*!"

"Like I said ..."

"Crap!" she said.

He crept backwards down the rickety stairs. Julie was the feisty one. Her two brothers were similarly occupied in other parts of the house. And he knew what they'd been thinking for the past month or so, ever since he'd had himself declared dead.

He was determined to do it. His lawyer told him it was stupid, and he knew his kids had thought he was nuts ever since they were little. "Dad's so strict! He never lets us do anything! Always preaching with his little moralistic stories. 'Instilling values.' It's not fair!" Even now, in their forties, they were still thinking like teenagers. But how they had loved their Mom. Of course, he had too, more than he could find words for. So when she passed away, and with the kids demonstrating how much they didn't need him, maybe even somehow blaming him, he figured, well, maybe he didn't need them anymore either. Still, it grieved him, this attitude of theirs. They were his, and a father's love craves action.

He waited until the Easter after Gloria's funeral, giving himself time to prepare, and then he made them all come to the summer house on Martha's Vineyard: Teddy, the eldest, a Hollywood producer, with his wife, Viola the Social Climber, and their three grumpy tweens. Julie, the outspoken PTA mom with her husband, Brad, an IT manager, who somehow seemed the smaller while actually being three inches taller than she, and two cowering elementary schoolers. Frank, the youngest and the one who at least tried to like him, a struggling accountant in Atlanta fresh from a divorce.

Everybody arrived about noon on Good Friday. There was polite small talk at first, then forced conviviality at dinner, but after they had adjourned to the living room it all poured forth.

"I can't believe you made us come all the way out here without telling us why," started Julie. "It's Spring Break and the only time we have off."

All the way from Boston. Eighty-five miles.

"Which is why I picked now, since school's out and it's a holiday weekend. Seemed pretty convenient to me."

"And that ferry is such a pain," joined Teddy. "Of course you know it's booked months in advance for this weekend. We had to charter a plane." Viola nodded vigorously as if they couldn't afford it, her way of reminding everybody that they could.

The five grandkids were out of earshot on the big front porch, engrossed in their iPhones and at least not fighting over anything.

"And yet you came."

"Well, the letter from your lawyer made it sound like life or death," offered Frank who had, in fact, booked ahead.

"Indeed."

He'd started them off with chilled Chardonnay and hors d'oeuvres followed by clam chowder. He'd grilled bacon-wrapped filet mignon to go with the catered tossed salad, lobster, corn on the cob, sautéed asparagus, and garlic mashed potatoes, washed down with Narragansett (a nod to his college days in Rhode Island) and topped off with apple pie à la mode, a perennial favorite on the Vineyard. A dinner to remember. He'd offered coffee and after dinner drinks, but no cigars.

Then his sated but still ungrateful family sat in the overstuffed leather-upholstered furniture he and Gloria had hauled over from New Bedford 30 years before. He stood by the fireplace with a Kahlua. Gas flames softly burnished the room's oak paneling. They looked at him with a mixture of disdain, apprehension, and feigned boredom. He wished he could take a picture.

"Here's how it is," he said. "Consider me dead."

Frank gasped quietly. Teddy smiled, obviously not getting it. Naturally, Julie spoke up first. He could have written her script, including stage directions, with no help needed from Teddy. First, the rolling of the eyes, and then …

"Dad, if this is another one of your harebrained schemes, we're leaving on the next ferry!"

"You can't," said Teddy. "It's been booked for months."

"Oh, shut up!"

Actually, it probably *was* a harebrained scheme, but he didn't think it advisable to present it as such. Score one for Julie anyway.

"So, uh, are you saying you have cancer or something, like Mom?" Frank blurted.

Julie put her hand to her mouth. The spouses looked at the floor.

29

"No, nothing like that. But thanks for your concern.

"Call me crazy," he continued, "and I know you already do, but it seems to me we don't need to carry our family charade any further. I've thought about this for a long time, so just listen for once. I love you, whether you believe it or not. All of you. Maybe you thought I wasn't there for you, but I did the best I could. I wasn't perfect, but who is? My own father was a good man, but he made mistakes too. I guess I just tried to do what I grew up seeing my father doing."

They were all shifting uncomfortably.

"You weren't really so bad," said Frank. The others gave obligatory nods of assent, but plainly everybody was waiting for a shoe to drop.

"So here you all are. On the whole it looks like you've turned out all right, if you do say so yourselves. And here I am. And there's this chasm between us. I don't know how it got there, and I've tried, but I can't cross it for the life of me. I've done all I can here, so I'm going to fast forward to the end."

"What does *that* mean?" said Teddy.

"Don't worry. You're going to like it."

"You're not going to kill yourself, are you?" said Julie, and immediately she put her hand to her mouth again. It would have looked good with a sock on it. "Sorry," she said quickly, "but you know what I mean."

"Maybe I do. But, no, I'm planning to stay healthy. If I kill myself then this won't work, and I want it to work."

They inched closer to the edges of their seats, which was not easy on slippery overstuffed leather upholstery, so he definitely had their attention.

"This is the one last thing I could think of to do for you."

He wasn't rich, but he'd done all right and his kids knew it. Maybe they were even a little bit proud of him, he wasn't sure. He'd had a good education and opportunities to advance, but he'd worked hard too, and he didn't squander what he'd earned. They'd put three kids through college, driven nice cars and taken a cruise now and then. The mortgages were paid up on the family home in Westchester and the house on the Vineyard.

"So here it is," he went on. "My bag is packed, and in a few minutes I'm heading for the ferry and I'll be gone."

He saw Brad mouth the words, "booked ahead." The others looked quizzical, but serious.

"You all know Matt Marklin, my lawyer. He'll be here in the morning to read you my will. I don't know the legalese, but in effect I've had myself declared dead, and so you will all be getting your inheritances early."

Their jaws dropped. He let the news sink in during a delicious moment of stunned silence. Before anybody could say, "You must be kidding," he went on.

"No, I'm not kidding. You already know you get equal shares of the estate, but you'll have to make decisions about who gets what when it comes to the furniture and household goods, and whether you want to sell the houses and cars. Oh, and the Sunfish. So you'll have to work together. And maybe learn something about trust. That should be fun."

They looked at each other.

"But … but you can't just *do* that!" said Frank. "Can you?"

"I can, and you shouldn't try to stop me. Frank, you're the executor of the estate, so it'll be up to you to keep things tidy."

"Gee, Dad, I don't know …" said Frank.

"Why him?" said Julie.

Viola shot her a look. He knew it meant, Leave well enough alone; we can talk Frank into anything.

"Well now, it seems like it's Christmas at Easter!" said Teddy, ever above it all.

"Frank's the CPA. He can use getting paid for his trouble, which the will provides for."

"I must say I'm ... surprised," allowed Julie, looking at her father without malice for the first time in years, but still with a trace of suspicion. "That seems very generous of you. Not that I've ever thought you were selfish or anything."

"Of course not."

"But ... why?"

"Someday maybe you'll understand. For now, just think of it as a gift that keeps on giving."

"What kind of answer is that?"

Teddy's turn again: "Are there any more surprises?"

"No, but there is a condition."

"I knew it," said Julie.

"You will have 90 days from tomorrow to complete the whole process of settling the estate. And I mean the *whole* process. After that, everything, and I mean all of it, not just what's not been settled, goes to charity. Think of it as a test."

Loud groans rose from the sofas and easy chairs and wafted out to the porch, catching the attention of the children. They scampered in from the gathering twilight to ask what was going on. He left it up to the grownups to come up with their own explanations. Most likely they'd just say, "Nothing."

He grabbed his suitcase from the hall closet and headed for the door without making further eye contact, a taxi already waiting. Amid unanswered cries of, "Is he really leaving?" and "Where's Grandpa going?" he left.

He knew it was a tough condition, the 90 days. Short notice, inconvenient, interrupting their precious agendas for a while. But wouldn't it have been almost the same if he had really died? Besides, he had put his affairs in order, and lawyer Matt knew where everything was and had already put the legal wheels in motion.

There was one more thing he suddenly remembered on the way

out, but he knew Matt would cover it on Saturday. After that night, if any of them saw him they were to ignore him, pretend he wasn't there, except of course to warn him of danger, like the house is on fire, or one of them was about to shoot him.

He didn't know how Matt had worked it out, but somehow all the institutions involved agreed, which meant the estate would be irrevocably passed on with no unexpected tax consequences, and he would be free of it. Even so, the kids would have to deal with more lawyers, the banks, insurance companies, real estate brokers, the IRS and all the other vultures who attend these events. But they were young. Why not get it over with now instead of 20 years down the road when they, too, would be feeling their ages? And there would be no funeral with sanctimonious eulogies and gloomy pall bearers.

The worst part would be going through both houses, floor by floor, closet by closet, drawer by drawer, bookcase by bookcase and old box by old box in two attics, two tool sheds and a garage, sifting and sorting, deciding what to keep and who would keep it, what to sell and what to give away and who to give it to. And then getting it all moved out. This he wanted to watch.

He had already removed all of his intimate personal effects. He'd switched wireless carriers, giving the new number only to Matt. With no close friends anymore, no one but the kids would really miss him, if even they did. He'd reserved enough money to live comfortably somewhere unknown even to Matt. For all practical purposes he was off the grid.

And he really did enjoy those 90 days. He'd crept through the houses refusing to help, like a reticent ghost while the kids toiled away in boredom and frustration.

They finished in time. Good for them.

Even better, from Matt's reports and what he sees on Facebook and Twitter, they seem to be doing well. The grandchildren too. Teddy's share gave him enough capital to start his own production company. He's won some awards, and he credits his father for his inspiration. Frank made some good investments with his share, and he's back on his feet, a partner in a thriving CPA firm. Julie had the hardest time, but she finally had to admit he did it right. No catch. No strings. Matt says she and the others are even beginning to tell their friends he was a good father.

They kept the Vineyard house, and they spend a lot of time there, together. Probably reliving childhood memories, the good ones anyway. Matt says the grandkids miss him. He misses them all. He remembers each birthday and anniversary with a card with no return address, and once in a while he sends Matt to deliver some advice he feels one of them might need. They can take it or leave it. Sometimes they take it. Sometimes they ask for more.

Matt says he thinks someday soon they will ask him to come back. Then, well, maybe he will. And that might really feel like Heaven.

Dr Barker's Scientific Metamorphical
Prostate Health Formula®

When Sam Gregory woke up one morning after an unusually restful night of sleep, he found he had become completely weightless. He was lying on his back but felt no solid support beneath him. When he lifted his head a little, he saw the covers, slightly dome-shaped, looking like they were about to slip off. It was almost as if he were floating. He could hardly keep from sliding out of bed, and it was only the weight of his pajamas and the little bit of friction between them and the sheets that held him in place.

"What's happened to me?" he thought. It was no dream. His room, the same room he had gone to sleep in mere hours before and that he shared with his wife, Gretchen, seemed no different from when he had put down his Kindle and switched off the lamp on his nightstand except that now sunshine poured in through the window, and Gretchen, habitually an early riser, was already gone.

On a table by the window was his sample case. Sam was a pharmaceutical salesman, or so he liked to think of himself. Actually, what he sold were nutritional supplements, chiefly the kind that claim to reduce the size of prostate glands in middle-aged men so they don't have to get up so often in the middle of the night to pee because their enlarged prostates crowd and thus reduce the capacity of their bladders. The sample case was open, and several bottles sat beside it on the table. One bottle was overturned, and an assortment of shiny brown capsules threatened to roll off onto the floor. A half-empty water glass stood next to the bottle.

It was so peaceful, Sam thought about going back to sleep for just a few minutes and in fact did so before he realized it. Moments later there was a knock on his door.

"Dad, aren't you up yet?" It was his 35 year old son, Adam, who had moved back in with them 14 years ago after graduating from college with a degree in philosophy and discovering the philosophy stores weren't hiring. "You were supposed to meet Dr Barker at Starbucks at eight, and you don't want to keep him waiting!"

Startled, Sam swung his legs over the side of the bed and tried to stand. This action caused him to spring up to the ceiling where he bumped his head and let out a yelp of surprise and pain before slumping back to the floor in a heap.

"What was that? Are you okay in there?"

"It was nothing," Sam replied, a little too quickly. "I stubbed my toe."

"It's almost eight-thirty!"

Wow, he *was* late! Uncharacteristically late. Usually he was up, showered, shaved and ready for breakfast by seven.

"Call Dr Barker and tell him I'm running a little behind this morning. I'll be out as soon as I can."

"You're sure you're okay?"

"I'm fine!"

Very slowly, Sam stood up again. How could he have been so careless as to sleep late, especially today when he had so much on his agenda? He knew it wouldn't sit well with his boss, Dr Barker, and certainly not with Gretchen and the ever-critical Adam, both of whom depended on him as the family's breadwinner.

He doffed his pajamas and, naked except for his gold wedding ring, took a step toward the bathroom, belatedly realizing as he again soared toward the ceiling that the pajamas were all that had kept him down before. Catching the ceiling with his hand just in time to avoid another skull-rattling collision, he gently eased back down and began pulling himself hand over hand from the bed to the dresser to the bathroom door and into the bathroom, much like the astronauts in the space station, except they wore space suits.

And, like a new astronaut, he felt a wave of nausea which lasted until he fixed his eyes on stable reference points in the room. He certainly didn't want to vomit, for fear it would float to the ceiling, giving a whole new meaning to the concept of throwing up.

Once into the bathroom and before showering, Sam performed some necessary ablutions. Although he had to hold himself down on the seat during the process, he was successful. This puzzled him.

He decided to experiment. He half-filled a glass of water from the tap. It had weight. What if he swallowed the water? Would that give him at least the water's weight as well? He downed the water and found he was still completely weightless. Odd. He half-filled the glass again and sipped generously from it, not swallowing this time. Still weightless. He spit it out into the sink. The water still had all its original weight.

So, anything inside his body would become weightless. Anything on his body, like clothing, still had weight. Anything eliminated from his body had weight. So he could still throw up and expect normal results, which was a relief, although the nausea had by now mostly passed.

How long was this going to last? How long would it take him to get used to the new sensations and learn the new rules that would be required if he wanted to keep his strange condition a secret? Did he want to keep it a secret? How had this happened in the first place? "And why to me?" he wondered.

After his shower, another adventure except he managed to keep his feet on the floor most of the time as long as he was wet, he dressed cautiously. The weight of his clothing helped keep him down, upright and reasonably balanced, but he had to work at it. He didn't want to start moon walking, leaping tall buildings, or moon landers, at a single bound. He practiced a somewhat mincing step. Not convincing. He had to do better than that or people would notice. Especially his family and Dr Barker.

He put on his heaviest shoes. His heaviest belt. His heaviest watch. A Zippo lighter went into his jacket pocket, although he hadn't smoked in years. He filled his pants pockets with loose change and hoped no one would notice the bulges. The coins would probably scratch his iPhone, but that was an acceptable risk. If he'd had a gun, he would have worn that too. He'd heard they were heavy.

Feeling a little more sure of his footing now, Sam made his way to the bathroom scale. It read 2 ½ pounds.

"Sam, are you up there?" It sounded like Dr Barker, calling from the bottom of the stairs! What was he doing here?

"What's going on?" Dr Barker called again. "It's not like you to be late."

Show time. Action and reaction, Sam kept telling himself as a reminder to time and power his movements very carefully. He still had mass and therefore inertia and momentum, but no weight because for some reason gravity didn't apply to his body today.

He opened the bedroom door and carefully stepped into the hall. He shuffled to the stairs and prepared to begin his descent. Everyone was waiting for him at the bottom. So far so good.

Then disaster. Stepping out from the landing, he misjudged his strength and found he had launched himself into the air, walking out into empty space like a cartoon character running off a cliff for some distance before an inevitable fall. Even with his 2 ½ pounds, he sailed out over the stairs for several feet before arcing to the bottom.

"Ed, what are you doing here?" Sam asked with a smile, acting as if nothing unusual had happened.

Everyone had noticed, of course, but what they had witnessed was so far from their experience it was almost as if they hadn't really seen it.

Dr Barker regarded Sam with a cross between a smile and a frown. Adam, standing behind Barker, was definitely frowning.

"I waited an hour for you at Starbucks. I called your cell, but there was no answer, so I got concerned."

Gretchen stood behind Adam with an expression of worry mixed with disappointment. "Your pancakes have gotten cold," she reported, "and your orange juice warm, I'm afraid."

Just then Frieda, Sam's mother-in-law who also had been living with them since Gretchen's father passed away about 10 years before, appeared behind Gretchen. She rolled her eyes but didn't say anything.

"And good morning to all of you too," said Sam. "Looks like it's going to be a nice day."

"Frankly, Sam, I'm worried about you," said Dr Barker. "Lately, you don't seem to have a heart for your work like you used to. Sales have been slipping, and the company can't afford that right now. We're all depending on you." Saying the last while looking around at the others.

"Well, thanks for sharing that with everyone, Ed," said Sam. "I'm sure we all needed the encouragement."

"There's no need to be sarcastic, Sam. We're all just a little upset because of our concern for you," said Dr Barker. "Let's go in the kitchen and talk. I want to make sure you're prepared for your appointments at the hospital today. You can still make the first one if we hurry."

Sam was a partner in the company, in fact one of only two. Dr Ed Barker, Ph.D., the inventor and patent-holder on all the products, was the other. All the manufacturing and shipping was contracted out so there were only a few employees, most of them clerical. It didn't take many people to run Barker Scientific Metamorphicals, Inc., and to market "Dr Barker's Scientific Metamorphical Prostate Health Formula" and the other products.

But Sam was the junior partner, which meant Barker could vote him out with a prearranged payoff any time he wanted. Barker had brought him into the business fifteen years ago after a short but promising career in advertising as a favor to Sam's late father-in-law and because his selling and people skills were much better than Barker's own.

And what Barker said was true. Sam wasn't as enthusiastic these days. The company's products, although profitable enough to provide him a salary sufficient to keep his family of four well fed and entertained, were—he had to face it—lackluster. Nothing very sexy about shrinking prostates even if it could ever be proven that the products actually worked.

The products were pretty standard for their type, principally saw palmetto but also measured proportions of zinc, pumpkin seed, grapefruit extract, beeswax, and a cocktail of other vitamins, herbs and spices variously thought to address not only prostate issues, but also the immune system, weight control, bad breath, canker sores, and possibly even cancer, depending on the pseudo-medical advice *du jour* dispensed in the popular press and afternoon TV doctor shows

Because Sam was still too young to have an enlarged prostate, he couldn't personally tell if the products had any effect, although he had tried them all, frequently and in large doses, because he wanted to be able to say he had when customers asked.

So Sam was selling hype and hope, and maybe false hope at that. Maybe it was time for a change.

Sam and Barker sat at the kitchen table. Gretchen offered coffee which Sam accepted, but Barker politely waved her away with a gesture toward his venti Starbucks Indivisible Blend™ Blonde Roast ("representing the spirit of America and helping to create jobs for Americans").

"These are still warm after all," said Sam, forking a pancake. "I see you used the 'feather light' batter mix. Really good."

Gretchen looked at him strangely but said nothing. She exited the kitchen, leaving Sam and Barker to carry on apparently undisturbed. No doubt she, Adam and Frieda were eavesdropping in the hall.

"This is a big day," started Barker.

"I know."

"Are you ready?"

"I've practiced my spiel on Adam, if that's what you mean, so I guess I'm as ready as I'll ever be. He didn't think it was so great, but he doesn't know the business, and anyway he doesn't think anything I do is so great, so it was par for the course."

"But what did *you* think?"

"It's passable."

"Too bad you don't have time to try it out on me," said Barker.

In fact, Sam wasn't sure just how passable it was. First of all, it was a strange assignment. Second, he wouldn't need to carry his sample case today. Ordinarily that might have been a relief, but today it meant less weight to help him keep his feet on the ground.

When he wasn't calling on giant retailers like Target and Walmart, an important part of Sam's job was to make sure the company's advertising slogan was true. The FDA was tough on nutritional supplements making unsubstantiated claims, so most of the industry relied on doublespeak that sounded plausible and scientific but really didn't say anything concrete.

For Sam's company, the slogan was "Nine out of 10 doctors in 10 big Midwest medical schools recommend products like Dr Barker's Scientific Metamorphical Prostate Health Formula for their patients who take nutritional supplements to relieve an enlarged prostate."

From his days in advertising, Sam knew it was nonsense, and so did nine out of 10 doctors, but Barker, who came up with it, insisted on using it, and the nine doctors didn't mind being paid to go along. Because 10 out of 10 doctors liked being paid for endorsements, it was the 10th doctor that was the problem. Sam's job was to visit the 10 big Midwest medical schools and convince every 10th doctor not to endorse the products. The prevailing wisdom (Barker's) was that having only 90% of the doctors endorse them made the company look honest.

Technically, it wasn't a hard sell. The 10th doctor would usually say something like, "I wouldn't endorse that stuff if you paid me! Wait, you are paying me. Now you say you don't want me to endorse it? That doesn't seem fair after I've been so loyal."

To which Sam would respond, "It's all right; we'll pay you more not to endorse it. Just keep it under your scrubs."

"Oh, well that's okay then. Where do I 'unsign'?"

Of course, word always leaked to the other doctors, and then most of them would want to become non-endorsers and make more money, which would have made for an awkward situation, truthful-slogan-wise. "No doctors in 10 big Midwest medical schools recommend products like Dr Barker's Scientific Metamorphical Prostate Health Formula for their patients who take nutritional supplements to relieve an enlarged prostate" just wouldn't have the same ring to it.

Sam had all he could handle repeatedly explaining the strategy of 90/10 endorsement equilibrium to the doctors, most of whom had no real head for business. Even so, the overall costs of the endorsement scheme kept rising as the company alternately made endorsing more lucrative than not endorsing and vice versa, depending on the shifting trends of doctor awareness of what was going on.

The real challenge was that there were so many doctors in the 10 big Midwest medical schools, hundreds in fact, plus there was about 20% turnover every year, and recruiting the new arrivals and keeping up with which ones endorsed and which ones didn't was tricky. Doctors kept jumping from the "endorse" column to the "not endorse" column and back based on the payment schedule, and Sam had to keep track of them and hold their hands when they threatened to defect. And he had to maintain up to date records documenting the magic nine-out-of-ten ratio the government watchdogs obsessed about.

Lately Sam had been thinking, Wouldn't it be easier to fix it so *all* the doctors in nine out of 10 big Midwest medical schools recommend the products and *all* the doctors in the 10th big Midwest medical school don't? Given, as it happened, that all 10 big Midwest medical schools had about the same number of doctors, the slogan would still be true, and a lot easier to keep track of. But he didn't think Barker would buy the idea.

"Look, I said I was sorry for being late, and I *am* sorry, so can we drop it?" said Sam, rising carefully from the table. "I do need to get going."

"Touchy, touchy," said Barker. "But you're right. I won't keep you much longer."

"What is it now?"

"Well … it's that flying down the stairs thing. Can you do it again?"

Sam minced toward the garage.

Returning home late that evening after enjoying a quick dinner at Chick-fil-A and welcoming the security of his car's seat belts, especially in the turns, Sam reflected on how well his appointments had gone. Or not. They were successful, yes, but not very satisfying.

43

The doctors he called upon all pretty much stuck to the script. Some, however, expressed moral or ethical reservations about endorsing the products. For those, Sam played the Hippocratic Oath card, quoting the part that says, "I will apply dietetic measures for the benefit of the sick according to my ability and judgment; I will keep them from harm and injustice." Since no one could see any harm or injustice in endorsing, Sam usually prevailed, especially if he paid in cash.

The only awkward moments involved using the hospital elevators. Forgetfully pushing the "Up" button with his accustomed force, even though it was with only one finger, he catapulted all 2 ½ pounds of himself clear across to the back of the car.

Fortunately, the jangling of loose change could barely be heard, and no one witnessed the spectacle. But then momentum and inertia came into play. Going up felt good, almost as if he had regained his normal weight for two seconds while the car accelerated, but he had to hold on tightly to the side rails so as not to be dashed against the ceiling when it stopped at each floor. Going down was terrifying, and it was all Sam could do to keep from riding on the ceiling all the way and dreading the moment when the car would stop and he wouldn't.

The family were all waiting for him when he came into the living room. Gretchen with a pout, the sour-faced Adam, and Frieda, on whose wrinkled face it was no longer possible to read expressions with confidence. Even Dr Barker was there. They had obviously been talking about him, but their body language showed they still had no explanation for his strange behavior. You could cut the silence with a knife.

"So, how was your day?" Gretchen ventured.

"Not bad. Yours?" Sam countered, easing into his usual chair, which he forbade anyone to call his Archie Bunker chair even though he knew they all did. He didn't make much of a dent in the seat cushion.

"Let's cut the crap, Dad," said Adam. "We want to know what's going on."

"This morning you were all 'concerned about me,' but now you make it sound like I'm keeping some big secret."

"Well aren't you?" said Barker.

"I guess I was, actually, but obviously it's out in the open now."

"Not really," said Adam. "All we know is you slept late, made strange noises in your room, and flew down the stairs."

They all laughed in spite of themselves at the way Adam had put it. Which broke the ice, at least.

"And all I know is I woke up this morning and I didn't weigh anything. I don't know why."

No one knew what to say.

"It feels pretty good, strangely enough, although at first it was hard to get used to, as you can imagine."

They couldn't imagine.

"Here, I'll show you something."

Sam stood up slowly, emptied his pockets, took off his watch and shoes, and gently launched himself through the air, landing on his hands. He held the handstand for several seconds before doing a triple back flip and twist, like a platform diver in the Olympics, this time landing upright if a little wobbly. Rising on tiptoe, he continued up, touching the ceiling with one hand before settling back to the floor.

The group stared in wide-eyed astonishment.

"You understand, if I didn't have any clothes on I could stay up there all day."

"How do you know that?" asked Gretchen.

"Trust me."

"I'm not sure I want to see that."

"I'm not sure you'll have much choice."

"We'll see about that," she retorted, her face reddening in a sideways glance at her mother. Frieda's expression remained inscrutable.

"Sam, is this going to affect your work?" asked Dr Barker.

45

"I don't see how, if I'm careful."

"One slip-up and we'll have people saying our products have a side effect we hadn't disclosed before. Weight reduction is one thing. But weightlessness? It's too risky."

"Don't worry, you could always get a job in the circus," said Adam.

Not that Sam hadn't been giving thought to a career change, even more so after this morning, but Circus Freak wasn't something he necessarily wanted on his résumé.

"No, that would involve even more travel than I do now. Maybe too much, don't you think?"

In fact they'd probably be happy if he travelled more, but he wasn't going to let Adam get to him.

"But ve could liff in Sarasota in za vinter," said Frieda.

After another twenty minutes of pointless conversation and a few more humiliating parlor tricks on Sam's part, he went up to his bedroom, closed the door and got ready for bed. He knew they were still talking about him downstairs. He more or less hovered over the bed reading his Kindle a while before slipping under the covers, tucking them in a little so he wouldn't accidentally slide out onto the floor during the night. He judged it was about 11:00 p.m. when he felt Gretchen slip silently into the bed on her side without turning on the light. The next morning he awoke to feel her getting up to go downstairs and start the coffee. He was still weightless.

Nothing changed, weightless-wise, for Sam during the next few weeks. He enjoyed that. More than once he slipped outside after everyone was asleep, took off his pajamas, slippers and wedding ring, and experimented. He floated over the deck behind his house, did somersaults as if he were on a trampoline, and flew into his neighbor's backyard, being careful not to be a peeping Tom or to be seen by anyone. Three nights in a row he spotted an owl in one of the trees apparently mesmerized by the sight of a human flying toward its perch. After overcoming some initial vertigo, Sam relished sitting atop the highest tree in the yard, a sturdy oak, imagining himself an owl, surveying his domain. He let his imagination run wild, a practice he had squelched years ago for seemingly more important pursuits.

Adam came out on the deck one night and saw Sam up in the tree.

"I thought I heard something," Adam said.

"You heard nothing. You saw nothing."

Adam went back in the house.

What had happened to Sam? What was causing this condition? Was it something he had eaten? Was it overdosing on the company's prostate health pills? (This was Dr Barker's fear.) Was it a magic spell, or was there a medical explanation? Would it run its course after which Sam would return to normal? Was there a cure?

Sam couldn't consult his regular family doctor without risking discovery, publicity and ruin, or in any case the potential ruin of the company. He and Barker supposed that, as with gunshot wounds, doctors would be bound to report such an unusual occurrence to the authorities. Or, his doctor might seize upon it as an opportunity to make a name for himself by writing it up for a medical journal. No, they had to be careful.

Sam had become especially friendly with one doctor at one of the 10 big Midwest medical schools and thought he could trust him. He made an appointment. Skeptical at first, but believing his eyes when Sam demonstrated a slow motion back flip off the examination table, "sticking" his ultra-soft landing, the doctor agreed to perform tests in secret. A new Sea-Doo would fit nicely in his garage.

Sam couldn't use his health insurance because "complete weightlessness" is not a recognized disease on the government's approved list. Barker grudgingly agreed to pay for the tests, and the Sea-Doo, with company funds. CT scans, X-rays, blood and urine analyses, allergy tests, and all manner of probing turned up nothing. Hypnotism was attempted to no avail; Sam remembered nothing pertinent. They decided to stop short of calling in an exorcist.

"I'm stumped," said the doctor. "I hope this doesn't change our deal, but I can't find anything wrong with him at all. Medically speaking, Sam is almost perfectly normal for a man of his age and should weigh about 185 pounds."

"Almost?" said Barker.

""Well, there is one thing. He doesn't have a prostate. And it looks like he never did."

"Thanks for doing no harm, Doctor," said Sam.

"No problem."

Over the next couple of months, Sam's condition still did not change.

But other things did. Gretchen barely spoke to him beyond the basic communication required by two people living in the same house and used to a routine that had been honed over 36 years of marriage. She continued to serve coffee and breakfast and usually had dinner waiting for him when he got home, but she herself was absent from the meal with increasing frequency, having joined not one but three evening book clubs.

Adam, who had usually greeted him at least half-heartedly when he appeared, now looked down at a book or newspaper or stayed lost in a TV show whenever Sam came in. Not that Sam didn't try.

"Anything promising in the want ads today, son?"

"Naw, just boring stuff I'm overqualified for. But I'll keep looking."

"What kind of work have you been looking for lately?"

"I haven't narrowed it down to one particular field, but it would sure be great to find a job as important and exciting as yours, Dad."

"Right. Well, I hope I haven't set the bar too high," said Sam.

"That's about the funniest thing since sliced bread."

Adam had been "looking" for work for as long as he'd been living at home and had even had a few interviews, mainly just to have something with which to keep his father at bay. Nothing ever came of them. His only apparent potentially marketable skill was a decent singing voice and some experience on the guitar from hours of playing "Kumbaya," "Where Have all the Flowers Gone?" and songs of similar ilk while trying to impress girls during college days. How to leverage it neither Sam nor Adam knew.

Frieda rarely spoke to him at all, but come to think of it that wasn't really a change.

Sam took to retiring to his bedroom after dinner. After a few weeks, he began taking his dinner into the bedroom with him and eating it there with his Kindle to keep him company, bringing out the dishes in the morning, rinsing them and putting them in the dishwasher.

Sometimes at night when they thought he was asleep, Sam would float out into the hall and listen in on their conversations about him. It was always the same: Apparently, Dr Barker had said more things to Gretchen that made her fear Sam would lose his job. Although they weren't rich, their financial condition had been stable until now. But Sam was no longer bringing home the bonuses they had gotten used to, and for him to be out of work completely ... well, that would spell economic disaster. Unpaid bills were already piling up. Sam felt like he was letting the family down.

Gretchen might have to find a job. Obviously, Adam would have to look for one in earnest.

One evening after dinner he surprised them by coming back downstairs to join their conversation, but they were less than receptive. Gretchen simply burst into sobs of frustration. Impulsively seizing a wine glass, she hurled it at Sam. He dodged, but it shattered against his forehead anyway, leaving a small cut. To the sound of tearful apologies, he retreated to his room, put on a Band-Aid, and went back to bed.

Most ominous were the changes at work. Dr Barker was weaning Sam away from face-to-face contact with doctors and retail customers. Then he forbade contact with suppliers. As a salesman, Sam didn't know exactly where this left him, except he couldn't see how he could contribute much to the success of the company if he couldn't go out and sell. He sat at his desk all day, occasionally answering the phone but mostly shuffling papers while listening to Barker's young secretary book appointments for a new man, Willy, whom Barker had hired.

Once, because he couldn't stand the boredom anymore, he floated out of his office and hovered over the secretary for a few seconds before sailing away toward the break room. It so freaked her out, since until that moment no one in the office but Barker knew of Sam's condition, that she screamed hysterically and threatened to quit. It took 10 minutes for Barker to calm the girl down, after which he called a staff meeting and let the cat fully out of the bag. After that, and a private dressing down Sam got from Barker, everyone avoided Sam when they could, except for a couple of guys in the mail room who thought it was "neat."

While things often looked up for Sam, so to speak, things were not looking good.

He worried.

And he thought.

Meditating in the wee hours in the treetops, sometimes with Kindle in hand, became his favorite pastime. Although he had lost whatever affection he once had for Dr Barker and no longer liked his job, and likely was seeing it disappear, he did love his family, much as they didn't appreciate him and never had. Maybe they'd be better off without him. What should he do?

An old Bible quotation kept popping into his mind. "Naked I came from my mother's womb, and naked I will depart. The Lord gave and the Lord has taken away; may the name of the Lord be praised." He looked it up. Job 1:21. It *would* be from the Book of Job. Perfect.

The long awaited blow finally came on the Monday before the Labor Day weekend. Dr Barker showed up at the house as Sam was having breakfast in the kitchen, alone except for his Kindle. On its screen was the front page of *The Wall Street Journal*, a trial subscription. Gretchen let Barker in and escorted him to the kitchen before withdrawing, but not out of earshot.

"This can't be good," said Sam.

"And good morning to you too," said Barker.

"Sorry, Ed. Coffee?"

"No thanks, I'm good," pointing to his tall Starbucks Reserve® Organic Galápagos San Cristóbal ("only a precious few coffees are deemed exceptional enough," and presumably helping to create jobs for San Cristóbalians).

"I should have known."

"But you're right, Sam. It isn't good."

"The coffee? But I thought ..."

"Never mind the stupid coffee! I've got bad news, Sam. Or maybe good news, depending on how you look at it."

"Let's hear it." But Sam knew what was coming, or most of it.

"Sam, this has been hard on everybody. Especially you, I know that. And I've thought this over for a long time because I didn't want to act too hastily, you know, in case your condition were to change."

"Go on."

"Well it doesn't look like it's going to change, and frankly, Sam, and I think you know this, you just haven't been pulling your weight at the office lately."

"Surely there must be a less indelicate way of putting that," said Sam.

"What? … Oh, oh yeah, well I'm sorry, I didn't mean it that way exactly, but, well, you do know what I'm talking about."

Sam did.

"You know I've had to hire and train somebody to take your place, and the company simply can't afford to pay you your salary just to answer phones and stack papers. I hate this, but I'm buying you out, Sam."

And there it was. If only Barker had given him the chance to prove he could somehow hide his condition from the people he came in contact with, not embarrass the company, and continue his good work. But Barker wasn't willing to take the chance. He made good on their contract and bought Sam's share of the company, handing him a cashier's check and giving him until Friday to clean out his office and leave.

The settlement money was substantial, but by no means enough to retire on while supporting a family.

Sam cleaned out his office. He left with mixed emotions. First, a feeling of relief. Part of him was glad Barker had made the decision for him. It was a decision he might have wanted to make himself, but how could he have explained it to Gretchen and Adam? And Frieda. He felt as if a great weight had been lifted, the irony of which his philosophy-minded son might have had fun dissecting.

The family took the news well at first, no doubt because they had been expecting it. Friday they carried on as usual, as if nothing had changed. But as reality set in, they knew this could be the beginning of a long trial. How long would the money last? With their budget already stretched, could the family economize even more for a while? Should Sam cash in his life insurance? Should they get a reverse mortgage? Where would Sam be able to find another job, even with a favorable reference from Barker? What should he, what could he, do now?

Saturday the household awoke to find Sam missing.

Had he gone out early for a walk? Had he gone to Starbucks to somehow recapture the illusion of interacting with other people in a way that mattered? Gretchen insisted Adam drive around the neighborhood for a while and look in at Starbucks, the Post Office, and the library, all places Sam had been known to visit from time to time. But there was no Sam. All his clothes were still in his closet and dresser in the bedroom. His coat was still in the hall closet. The only fresh, telling, and sad traces of him were his pajamas, his slippers, his wedding ring, and his Kindle. Sam was gone.

Frieda went back to her room. Adam was unusually silent. Clutching Sam's ring, Gretchen went to the kitchen and stared out the window for a long time.

"I did love him," she whispered, aware that Adam had slipped quietly into the kitchen behind her.

"I know," he said.

"Once."

* * *

The airliner was still at 30,000 feet but preparing for its descent into Omaha when the captain noticed something out the window.

"What the heck is that?" he said.

"Where?" said the first officer.

"There! About 11 o'clock. Do you see it?"

"No, I … wait, now I see something. Hard to make out though."

"What does it look like to you?" asked the captain.

"I have to say it looks like a naked man."

"That's what I thought too. Look, his arms are stretched out like he's flying. Which I guess he is."

"Up here your eyes do play tricks on you, don't they?" said the first officer. "I once thought I saw Amelia Earhart's plane in the distance, but it turned out to be just a normal UFO."

"Yeah, you're right."

"Right. So here's the test."

"Yes?"

"Is he wearing a cape?"

Laughing, the captain disengaged the autopilot and the plane slowly turned away.

* * *

For some reason, Adam thought to pick up Sam's Kindle and see what kind of books and stories were on it. What had Sam been reading? Surprisingly, or maybe not, it was uplifting stuff. Stories of love and optimism, about people triumphing in adversity, even religious stories about God helping people overcome their circumstances and live victorious, significant lives.

Adam had an idea. "It's a holiday weekend," he announced to Gretchen and Frieda. "Let's go on a picnic!"

At first the women were aghast at the thought, but Adam kept insisting, and eventually they came to look on it as maybe a healthy diversion from the misery they had been enduring for so many months. So they went to the park. Gretchen didn't feel like cooking, so they stopped by Chick-fil-A on the way. Adam brought his guitar.

Adam invited Dr Barker, and after some initial reluctance, he came too, with his wife and two children. He brought the drinks. Adam asked Frieda to go find some ants, assuring her they were an important component of any American picnic. She didn't get it.

They had fun.

Dr Barker asked Adam if he would consider stopping by the office the following week to talk about a job. Adam said he would, although he knew it was probably a long shot. But he'd heard good things about Barker's secretary.

* * *

Epilogue

I want to thank Walt Pilcher for letting me write this story under his name. I felt it needed to be written as fiction first because no one would believe it if it were reported as fact. The tabloids would have exploited it to the fullest: "Balloon Boy Loses Balloon!" "Lawnchair Larry Rides Again, This Time Chairless!" "Tall Buildings and Kryptonite No Match for this Capeless Crusader!" Stuff like that.

It was bad enough the airline captain's story got on "Good Morning America" after his teenage son, upon hearing his father tell about the sighting, faked a cockpit voice recorder transcription of the dialogue between him and the first officer and put it on YouTube. I saw the show but said nothing to Mom and Grandma. Fortunately, it didn't go viral and after enjoying their 15 minutes of fame the captain and his son quickly slid back into obscurity along with the story.

Anyway, people in our neighborhood and at Dad's company have been asking what happened to him since he disappeared, and we can't put them off much longer with stories of extended vacations and family funerals in distant cities. I thought if people could just get used to the idea first as "fiction," they would be better prepared to accept it when the truth finally came out from a respected source.

Oh, and believe me, my dad wasn't full of hot air, or helium, as some will suggest. His voice sounded perfectly normal the whole time.

I know what happened to my father, Sam Gregory, at the end.

It was the middle of the night. It was dark. I was up late watching TV, and I guess he assumed I was asleep. Or maybe he didn't. I sometimes wonder. Anyhow, I thought I heard something out on the deck and went to investigate. I had seen him there before, of course, usually from my darkened bedroom window, but one time I actually went out and caught him sitting (if that's the right word) up in that oak tree, as if surveying his domain, like an owl. This time was different. Something told me he wasn't coming down. By then I don't know what the concepts of "up" and "down" meant for him, but it was certainly "down" to me.

"Come down, Dad. Please."

"I can't, son."

"But you must. We're depending on you."

"I know. That's just it. I can't provide for you anymore. Maybe this way is better."

"No, I don't mean we just depend on you for money. You're our anchor. We know you love us. We love you too, Dad."

"It's too late."

"Dad, I know I've disappointed you. I know you told me to major in something more practical, like business administration. But I really will try to find a job."

"I believe you will. And maybe a wife too."

Then he stood up on top of that highest tree branch and crouched as if to spring off it.

"No, don't do it! Yes, I'm a philosophy major, but I also took physics in high school. If you launch yourself, weightless, into the air with no tether or anything to grab onto you'll simply continue to go up in the direction you started, and nothing will stop you. Air resistance may slow you down, but your momentum will keep you going up and up until there's no more air. You'll die!"

"Maybe. But oh, the places I'll go. The things I'll see."

Then Dad launched himself straight up. There was nothing more I could say except, "Goodbye."

"Goodbye, Adam."

I watched him rise. I watched him get smaller and smaller against the starlight. Until finally I couldn't see him anymore.

Adam Gregory

Epi-epilogue

I don't believe a word of that story. It's preposterous and much too derivative, except for the airliner part. Anyway, please do not send me job opportunities for "Adam Gregory."

Walt Pilcher

Caveat Aegrotus (Let the Patient Beware)
A Medical Cautionary Tale in Verse

I. Warning

The salesman sells, the lion tamer tames,
the Jell-O gels, the broker brokers shares,
and some purveying services and wares
perversely play low appellation games.
Inherent urge, a mindless bent to do,
so builders build and plumbers plumb for pay,
and surgeons "surge" and dentists "dent" away,
mere titles driving actions they pursue.
Beware their lust to justify existence,
insisting we at once comply like sheep.
Proud expertise demands a price too steep
and denigrates with arrogant persistence
more common sense solutions while our claims
to health and wealth and worth go down in flames.

II. Object Lesson (a true story)

The swollen lymph node rose within my arm.
Had cancer or infection made it grow?
The Hippocratic Oath says, "Do no harm;"
the doc said, "Take it out and then we'll know."

"Whoa, not so fast," I cried with some alarm.
"Suppose it's just a virus sneak attack,
and though my node be working like a charm
I don't believe you plan to put it back."

"New plan," he said. "Instead I'll give it time
to work its way to normal size again
before I pluck it from you in its prime
and put you through unnecessary pain."

Take heed the eager surgeon to disarm.
Consider this before you buy the farm.

How to Attract a Man

And you thought osmium was the densest element on earth?

"That was really odd," said Alice, carefully placing her Styrofoam cup on the table and taking a seat across from Ginger.

"What was?" asked Ginger, hoping for something juicy.

The two women hadn't seen each other much in the five years since college but had recently met by chance in the employee cafeteria, happily discovering they both worked for the same company. Now they often met here on break.

"I got asked a question today that I hadn't given much thought to until now" said Alice. "It's been bugging me ever since." She sipped and made a face. The coffee was lukewarm.

"Well …?"

"It was Fred, the guy from Accounting who always seems a little lost."

"Oh yeah, I know Fred. I see him in the hall sometimes, and he seems nice."

"He's shy," Alice continued, "but lately he's been acting like I'm the sister he maybe never had."

"What did he say?"

"He wanted to know what women do to attract men."

"My gosh, you mean he doesn't know?" exclaimed Ginger.

"Well apparently he doesn't get out much."

"What did you tell him? I hope you didn't give away any secrets!"

"Oh, do we have secrets?" Alice asked, shooting Ginger a look. They both smirked.

"Anyway, why not?" Alice went on. "I think he's harmless enough, and the poor guy seemed desperate to know. What would *you* have told him?"

Ginger took a slow sip from her own cup. "You know, I'm not sure. It's not something I've thought a lot about since college."

"Maybe that's why you're still single."

"Oh thanks. Need I remind you, you're still single too?"

"Sorry, low blow."

"Anyway, things were different in college," said Ginger. "It didn't take much to attract a man."

"But these days," said Alice, "men – what do they really want?"

"Exactly! And now it's going to be Frieda Freud to the rescue?"

"Quit beating around the bush. What would attract a man?" Alice persisted.

"I guess the first thing is to make him notice me – in a good way, of course, regardless of my looks, although that's important too. I'd always want to look my best."

"And …?" prompted Alice.

"Well, I think if I complimented him on something it would get his attention."

"I agree with that. What else?"

"Maybe show an interest in something I know he's interested in," continued Ginger.

"How do you find that out?"

"If you don't know by observation then I guess you just ask him. That in itself would make a good impression, wouldn't it? Or maybe you could ask his friends … although that might be awkward. You don't want anybody to think you're on the make. But I'm doing all the talking here. What did you tell Fred?"

"Are you ready for this?" asked Alice.

"Ready for what? What are you talking about?"

"I told him all the things you just said."

"Uh oh," said Ginger. "Then what?"

"He said the strangest thing. He said, 'You know that girl, Ginger, you hang around with? She's been doing all that. Do you think there's something going on?'"

An Old Score

An Interactive Short Story – *You* Choose the Ending!
(Multiple or compound endings permitted)

In his office five stories above the hot, stinking city pavement, Ellery Doyle sat behind an ornate desk fashioned of wood from a German cruiser his great grandfather's ship had rammed during the War. He whistled to himself and whittled with a pocketknife on an empty Dixie cup from the water cooler by the door. His cigar now cold, he had stopped nervously blowing smoke rings at the large green "Kryptonite" snow-globe paperweight his sister had purchased at the Warner Brothers store on a trip to Los Angeles. An ancient Smith-Corona Clipper typewriter sat in a corner, a hand-me-down from his father's college days. Doyle occasionally used it for short reports, but ink ribbons were hard to find so mostly it gathered dust, perched on its little table as if waiting for a call from the Smithsonian.

"11:30 a.m.," said the wall clock.

"Private," said the frosted glass on the door.

"I am a Bigelow," said the carpet on the floor.

"Doyle Investigations," said the tasteful hand painted sign on the building.

"QWERTYUIOP¼" said the Smith-Corona.

The intercom on Doyle's desk buzzed. It was Lois, his longtime secretary and sometime squeeze.

Business was slow. Not much to investigate in a small town, even one with hot, stinking city pavement, but there were signs of growth—new buildings springing up here and there, like mushrooms. Meaning eventually more fodder for both him and the police. Meanwhile, still time for a little golf. Maybe some squeezing. He pressed the intercom button.

"Detective de Tocqueville is here to see you, sir," calling him "sir" in front of clients and guests.

"And right on time," he answered, frowning. "Send him in. I'm afraid Detective de Tocqueville and I have a score to settle ..."

Inner tension mounting quickly, he accidentally nicked his thumb with the pocketknife. He hardly noticed the resulting trace of blood as he set the cup and knife down on the desk blotter and let his gaze wander to the M1 Garand rifle he kept behind the window drapes to his right, a gift from an uncle. He patted its butt lovingly and then turned as the door opened.

"11:31 a.m.," said the clock.

"etavirP," said the frosted glass.

"I am a Bigelow," said the carpet.

"ASDFGHJKL: @" said the Smith-Corona.

"Doyle Investigations," said the tasteful hand painted sign.

"Good morning, Ellery," said Detective de Tocqueville.

Glaucon de Tocqueville stepped into the office, closed the door behind him, and stood facing Doyle, his gaze carefully taking in his surroundings. He was a big man, a twenty-year veteran of FBI and police work, and he carried himself well. When he spoke in anger, which was often, it was as if Goliath had grabbed the slingshot and was asking David what he was going to do for an encore.

"You're looking agreeable this morning, Glaucon," said Doyle, managing a smile. "Have a seat. I guess this business can't wait any longer."

"You're not just whittling Dixie there, Ellery," enjoined de Tocqueville, declining a chair.

"Very funny."

Silence passed between the two men for a long moment.

"11:32 a.m.," said the clock.

"neM," said the door.

"I am a Bigelow," said the carpet on the floor.

"ZXCVBNM,.?" said the Smith-Corona.

"Doyle Investigations," said the tasteful hand painted sign.

"Squeeze me," said Lois, out of earshot.

"Look, I didn't come here to discuss your hobbies," said de Tocqueville finally.

Doyle rose from his swivel chair and slowly walked around the desk as he gathered himself to speak, never going beyond easy reach of the gaudy snow-globe. He concentrated on making his voice sound firm and unwavering.

"I know you're a man of few words, Glaucon, and so am I. I also know we don't trust each other, so let's just lay our cards on the table and get this over with. I have a detective agency to run here."

"So *you* say. All right, Doyle, I want to know about the 13th!"

"I have an alibi for the 13th! You know that! We've discussed this." His voice was steady.

De Tocqueville sighed. "Okay, never mind about the 13th for now. I'm really more interested in the 16th anyway."

"Do you honestly still believe there was foul play on the 16th, de Tocqueville?"

"We both know there was."

"But why make a Federal case out of it?"

"Very funny."

Suddenly, Doyle snatched up the snow-globe and angrily hurled it out the open window. De Tocqueville peered over the sill in time to see it shatter on the hot, stinking city pavement, green shards of "Kryptonite" flying everywhere. Turning back, he caught sight of the M1, now partly revealed under the windowsill.

"Nice piece," he said.

"Just blanks, but scares the crap out of the pigeons!" piped Doyle, pleased that the other man appreciated at least one of his interests in spite of his earlier expression of disdain.

"But it won't do you any good to change the subject, Ellery. The fact is, you owe me a hundred bucks. You thought I didn't see your clumsy 'foot wedge' on 16. You'd have had a double bogey if you'd played it straight. So pay up!"

Doyle sat down limply and looked up at Detective de Tocqueville with resignation.

"You win, I guess," he said. Then he brightened. "But maybe we can work out a deal!"

"Oh, yeah? What kind of deal?" asked de Tocqueville.

"How about a free investigation?"

"Listen, you have information for the police, it better be free!" slipping easily into the familiar obligatory private eye versus real police detective repartee the two had traded grudgingly for years.

"Will you take a check?'

"From you?"

With a sigh, Doyle opened a desk drawer and removed a tooled leather cash box, a gift from his mother on the tenth anniversary of his agency's opening. He unlocked it, took out a bill, and handed it to de Tocqueville.

"About time, too," said de Tocqueville, "and knowing you, I'll bet you want a receipt."

"Well ..."

"Well, forget it! Type one up on that old Smith-Corona there and sign it yourself. By the way, has the Smithsonian called about that thing yet?"

"No need to be sarcastic."

"Just asking," said a grinning de Tocqueville, turning to leave.

"Are we still on for the 21st?"

"You bet, especially if there's no break in this case I'm working on. I'm sick of pounding the hot, stinking city pavement for leads that go nowhere."

"Anything I can help you with?"

"Never mind that. Just be there on time with your usual supply of extra balls." With that, Detective de Tocqueville departed.

"11:36 a.m.," said the clock.

"ylnO tixE ycnegremE," said the door.

"I am a Bigelow," said the carpet.

"Eat Me," said the tasteful hand painted sign.

Ending One

Alice picked up the tiny five-story building as if it were a mushroom and read the tasteful hand painted sign. Her feet were sinking into the hot, stinking city pavement, green shards of something pricking her ankles. It was truly disconcerting, she thought, never to know from one moment to the next what one's size was going to be.

"I wonder whether, by eating this tiny building, I might possibly grow small again …"

Ending Two

Superman stared at the buildings that had sprung up like mushrooms since his last visit.

"I must be getting old," he thought. "These buildings always seemed shorter before. Easier to leap in a single bound. Now it takes two, sometimes three bounds. And what's all this green stuff?"

Ending Three (Prerequisite: Must first choose Endings One and Two)
Superman stared up at Alice. Then he stared down at Alice.

Ending Four

The intercom buzzed once again. Doyle pressed the button. "Sorry, sir, but you really need to take this call," Lois announced. "It's the Smithsonian."

Ending Five (Prerequisite: Must first choose Endings One, Two and Three)

Alice and Superman sat across from at each other over their half-caf caramel lattes at Starbucks discussing old times, momentarily unmindful of the hot, stinking city pavement with its strange green shards.

"So, Supe … may I call you Supe? It seems an apt appellation for the times. And I must say, you do look well. Have you any news from Lois of late?"

"Not much, Al. She married a local private eye, took up golf. I was too busy and too tired to go to the wedding. Just couldn't squeeze it in. Otherwise, you know I would have leaped at the chance."

"Of course; such a pity. By the way, have you any plans for this coming Friday evening? If I might suggest, there is a new restaurant at the mall and I am given to understand that they serve a passable Portobello."

Self Rising

The bake-off judges approached, their mouths watering. The layer cakes towered arrogantly over their lesser baked brethren – the pies displaying wide-eyed innocence against the moment the test slices would be taken, rendering them Pac-Man-like and hungry looking; the lowly cookies cowering like oversize poker chips waiting to be wagered, or redeemed; and the brownies lurking darkly, their crackled top glazes dully reflecting the flickering fluorescent ceiling lights of the church fellowship hall. All awaited their separate ordeals under the watchful eyes of their creators and the few peckish hangers-on who had pledged their donations for tasty crumbs. Granny Martha, a lifelong church member who had won the bake-off almost every year since anyone could remember, sat smugly with her coterie in the nearest corner of the room where the view was best and where the judges could not fail to be aware of her brooding presence.

"What am I doing here?" Linda's inner voices screamed. "How did I ever let Steffie talk me into this?"

Brows furrowed and pens poised, the judges came down the line, inexorably nearer to Linda's entry.

At least it would be over soon, and it was probably just as well Dan couldn't be here to see it.

"Don't get me wrong," Linda's mother, Mae, had said in the kitchen one morning several months earlier. "Your father and I love having you live with us, especially since you're paying rent and doing the dishes, but, honey, you do need to get out more. You know, meet new people ..."

It was the familiar start to a conversation Mae had begun countless times since Linda had moved back in at the age of 29 after her husband had left her for a full time vacation in Aruba.

"I'm just not ready yet, Mom. I've told you a million times. I'll get back on my feet soon."

"We only want what's best for you, Linda, you know that."

"Yes I do, Mom. I do," she said, kissing her mother on the forehead. "And even though I got downsized at the bank, the new job is fine and maybe one of these days I'll get a raise and then I can afford my own place. Anyway, I gotta go."

The divorce settlement was a meager supplement to Linda's wages as a clerk and bookkeeper at the Bread Box Bakery where her longtime friend, Steffie, had given her a job. That was only a stop-gap economic refuge until she could find a "real" job more suited her degree in political science from State, with a minor in accounting. Her résumé got her some promising interviews, but for some reason she rarely got a call back. A show of optimism, especially around her mother, was better than giving in to the quiet desperation Linda often felt deep down.

"Are you coming home right after work?"

"Yes, Mom." She was out the door and into her blue Miata.

The car was her only concession to luxury. It wasn't an expensive car, but it was snappy and sporty nonetheless. It said, "Look at me!" without the risk of anybody actually doing it long enough that she'd have to interact with them. Vroom-vroom, and away. And besides, it was like taking a ten minute vacation to and from work.

She parked behind the bakery so as not to deprive customers of the more convenient spaces in front. The aromas were good as she came through the back door and stashed her purse under her desk.

"Bear claws and donuts today!" yelled Steffie from the combination store and coffee shop up front, where a few people were already sipping lattes in the white wrought iron chairs, some with their laptops open on the little round tables. Free Wi-Fi.

"I'll be right out," answered Linda. She put on her apron and name badge and joined Steffie behind a display counter full of assorted pastries, breads and muffins and other treats. "You amaze me," she said to Steffie.

"What do you mean?"

"How you can bake all this stuff every day and work the counter too, all without breaking a sweat."

"You should have seen the sweat when I was first getting started! I was afraid some of it would fall on the recipes."

"Wouldn't have done them any harm. Uh, not that they needed any improvement of course. I'm just saying ..."

"I know. And I *am* constantly trying to improve them. Don't want the customers to get bored."

"So, they're sort of like your children in a way?" said Linda.

"Who, the customers or the donuts?"

One of the customers looked up, and then looked away quickly.

"The ... Oh, never mind. You know what I mean," stammered Linda.

"Well, sometimes I do," said Steffie. "But anyway I've done a lot less sweating since you came on board."

"I wish I could believe that ..."

"Oh, believe it!"

A couple of customers got up, tossed their trash into the receptacle by the front door, and waved goodbye to Steffie as the bell over the door tinkled merrily.

Another man, the one who had looked up, approached the counter. "Say, Steffie, can I have a bear claw to go?"

71

"Sure, Dan. Oh, Linda, can you help him? I've got to get some dough out of the fridge."

"I always thought you got your dough from the bank," said Dan.

"Ha-ha. Listen, Linda here used to work in a bank, and I don't think she ever brought home much dough," said Steffie.

"Well maybe she just wasn't *pun*-ctual enough," he said.

What a jerk, thought Linda. Besides, it had been a lot more "dough" than Steffie was paying her. Not that she wasn't grateful. Her eyes narrowing, she rang up the purchase with no more conversation than was necessary. Dan thanked her and left.

Did I just get the cold shoulder in there, Dan wondered, or was something else going on? That girl was snooty. Not the right attitude for a bakery. But she was efficient. Kind of pretty too.

Dan's mind wandered to the next items on his list for the morning. First, off to Murph's Hardware for some varnish. Then to the Post Office to see if his guitar strings had arrived, and finally to the music store for a look at a new line of dreadnought cases. "I do love the shapes and sounds of a guitar," he mused. Not unlike a woman's.

After the morning rush and before the lunchtime crowd, usually including a couple of policemen who claimed they were just keeping up appearances, Linda and Steffie had a few minutes alone in the back room where Linda did the bookkeeping.

"We should talk," said Steffie.

Linda looked up from her work with some alarm. Had she said something to offend Steffie? Was Steffie going to cut her hours, or maybe even let her go, in spite of what she'd said earlier?

"I know you think I hired you out of charity or something," Steffie started, speaking softly in case someone had come in unnoticed out front.

"Of course not," said Linda, flushing.

"But I didn't. I wouldn't. When you lost your job at the bank I have to say I *was* glad in a way."

"What! You must be kidding!"

"Sorry, that was a bad way of putting it. I did feel bad for you and was sorry it happened, because you're my friend. But from a purely selfish point of view, it was an opportunity for me. I need you, Linda. I really do. I wasn't kidding about the sweat."

"I'm a little confused."

"I'm good at baking," said Steffie. "And I love dealing with the customers. But the paperwork drives me crazy! My husband helped for a while, bless him, but he has a job too and travels a lot, and it just wasn't working out. We couldn't tell if I was making any money or if this was just going to be a very expensive hobby."

"Why didn't he ask you to close up then?"

"Bill? Why? Bill would never do that. He's been unbelievably supportive. What he said was, 'Hire somebody to help you.'"

"Really?"

"Yes. And I hired you. And I'm glad, and you need to know that. In less than a month you straightened the books out. For the first time, I know where we stand. And you have great ideas on how to get publicity and how to run specials, and lots of other things I don't have a head for. We make a really good team, I think."

"Gosh."

"I'm sorry I can't pay you more right now, but you've seen the numbers. Even though the business is growing, we're not putting much money in the bank yet. Or 'dough,' maybe."

"I do understand," said Linda.

"So I just thought we should get that straight. I don't do charity cases, unless it's church work or something. Look at me: I ... need ... you! Okay?"

"Okay."

"Good! I'm glad that's settled. Now there is just one thing ..." continued Steffie.

Uh-oh, thought Linda.

"You need to learn how to bake."

"If you weren't kidding before, you must be now," cried Linda. "You don't do charity, and I don't bake!" Trembling, she stood up and practically ripped off her apron, flinging it onto the desk.

"Whoa, girl! I must have pushed a big button there," said Steffie. "Didn't mean to."

"I ... I'm sorry. It's just ... it's just, I guess I'm just fed up with people wanting to tell me what to do with my life. My mother. My friends. My ex-husband. My supervisor at the bank. It never stops."

"I'm not qualified to run your life, Linda. I can barely manage my own. I'm only saying it might be fun to learn something new. Like canoeing or golf. I like baking so much, I tend to assume everyone else would like it too, and I want to share it."

"Thanks, but I'm really not interested right now," said Linda, more calmly this time.

Sensing she could take it a little further, Steffie tried again. "Have you ever baked anything?"

"Of course I have!"

"When?"

"In Home Ec in high school we had to bake something."

"And ...?"

"I did okay with my little brownies, and we put them in a box with what the other girls made and passed them out to the boys at football practice, and I got an 'A,' and I brought a brownie home for my father, and he said, 'Yum, yum' ... and I hated every minute of it! So phony!"

"Is that when all this started? I mean the feeling that people were trying to run your life?"

"Yes, maybe it was. Everything was all about getting ready to be a 'good wife and mother.' It was never about finding myself, or exploring what other opportunities might be there."

"So Women's Lib did a number on you at about that time, maybe?"

"It didn't *do a number* on me. It made me see very clearly. Do you remember the magazine ad for some kind of flour where the 'little housewife' is standing there in her party dress and high heels and a cutesy little apron, and she's holding out a basket of biscuits or something, looking soooo pleased as if to say, 'Look at pretty little me; didn't I do good? Pat me on my pretty little head'?"

"Yeah, I think so," said Steffie. "Self-rising flour if I recall."

"Well, that's when Betty Crocker became my enemy!"

"Wow, this runs deep."

"Yes it does."

"So, as far as you're concerned, baking is 'women's work,' and you're not about to be pigeonholed, is that it?"

"Yes, that's about right. And no offense to you, because you do it as a business, and that's different." Linda sat back down.

"And bookkeeping isn't 'women's work'?"

"Maybe it used to be, but plenty of men do it now too."

"But baking doesn't qualify in your book because not very many men do it, is that what I'm hearing?"

Linda thought about that for a moment. "Well, when you put it that way, it sounds kind of stupid. You're twisting my meaning …"

"No, I'm not really. But let's say, just for discussion proposes, that lots of men bake. Would you try it then?"

"Actually, I thought it was kind of fun. The baking itself, I mean. Not the other part, with the football players and pleasing Daddy and everything."

"Now we're getting somewhere!" said Steffie.

"But I'd be no good at it. Not after all these years."

"Nonsense!" said Steffie. "Like riding a bicycle – you never forget."

The bell over the front door tinkled, and two policemen came in.

"You guys are early," shouted Steffie. "I'll be right out!" Then, to Linda, "We'll finish this later, okay?"

"Just one question."

"All right, but hurry. The cops are hungry."

"Next you'll probably tell me that that guy, Dan, bakes."

"Ahhh yes … Dan," said Steffie with mock thoughtfulness, "… I don't really know."

That evening over dinner, Linda asked Mae rather timidly if she would be willing to share any of her recipes.

"Well, I probably would, but why do you need recipes all of a sudden?" asked Mae.

"Steffie thinks it would be good for business if I could bake a few things once in a while," said Linda, sugar coating the truth just a little.

"But, Linda, honey, you don't bake," said Mae.

"That brownie you brought home from high school was pretty good, I thought," said Linda's father.

"Yes, it was," agreed Mae, who had had a bite of it herself, "but that was, what, over ten years ago?"

"Thanks, Dad," said Linda, ignoring her mother's remark. This was going to require perseverance. "Steffie wants to teach me."

"Doesn't she have any good recipes you could use?"

"She has great recipes, but I think some of yours are even better."

"Why, thank you, dear."

"And they're different from hers, so they'll add variety. She's looking for more of that."

"Well, what kind of recipes do you want? Brownies? Cookies? My coffee cake you've always liked so much? Angel food cake? Devil's food cake? Lemon squares? Key lime pie?"

Was Mae trying to embarrass her or just be extra helpful?

"How about all of those? Then when I get with Steffie maybe I'll start with the brownies since at least I've done those before."

Over the next few weeks, between customer rushes, Linda became an apprentice baker at the Bread Box. With Mae's recipes, Linda tried her hand, first with brownies, but then with other items as well. The first few attempts weren't disasters, but they weren't ready for prime time either. Sometimes the batter was still too lumpy when Linda put it in the oven. Once she mistook salt for sugar. Some of Mae's recipes were quite old, handed down from a time before modern ovens, so they had to be adjusted, with inconsistent results.

Linda tried using self-rising flour, and the results were better and seemed acceptable to Steffie, but still she wasn't satisfied.

"What's the problem?" Steffie asked one day when Linda got back from delivering the results of her day's experiments to the nearby Senior Center, looking glum.

"It's just too predictable," said Linda.

"What, life or baking?"

"No, I mean the self-rising flour solved my main problems, and the results are good, but I want them to be better."

"I didn't realize you were such a perfectionist, or so competitive," said Steffie.

"I didn't either, and I'm not trying to compete with *you*, of course."

"Of course," said Steffie with a laugh. "But ..."

"Well, I just think I can do better."

"Got any ideas?"

"It's the flour, isn't it?" asked Linda.

"Meaning what?"

"Self-rising flour is just regular flour with some baking powder and salt added, right?"

"Right," said Steffie.

"The baking powder and heat control how much the dough rises. That's the leaven, sort of like yeast, and the salt is for flavor."

"And ..."

"Well, if I use self-rising flour from a box, the proportions of flour, salt and baking powder are the same every time. So I get plain old good results, which anybody can get, but not great results. Maybe I should be making my own self-rising flour so I can vary the proportions and the baking times and temperatures and see what happens."

"Uh-oh, now you've discovered my secret," said Steffie.

"You mean that's what you do? Why didn't you just tell me?"

"I was getting around to it, but you needed to learn the basics first."

"Oh, thanks a lot!"

"You can thank me later. For now, let's just let you go make some flour."

Linda experimented. Eventually, after a few more fits and starts, some of Linda's creations were finding their way into the display case, and people were buying them. She challenged herself to try unusual items, such as a pear and almond torte, a favorite treat she had discovered during a college semester in Paris. Steffie praised it, and it sold quickly, so Steffie started offering it on a regular basis.

Dan came in often, drank his morning coffee over a newspaper, and made off with a bear claw to go, sometimes two. No wisecracks, just very businesslike and polite. Occasionally, Linda noticed him stopping in during the afternoon to share a word or two with Steffie while Linda worked on her bookkeeping in the back. More than once she caught him glancing toward the back room, but their eyes never met. Sometimes he bought something she had baked, but she doubted he knew that unless Steffie had told him. He had a nice smile. Strangely, she found herself wishing he would open up more, bring back the puns, awful as they were. She was sorry she had been so rude.

"I hope you're pleased with how well your stuff is selling," said Steffie one evening as they were closing up.

"Oh, they're just buying it because they assume you baked it," said Linda.

"Do you really think I would risk my reputation by putting substandard goods out here?"

"Well, maybe not, but I know you're just trying to be encouraging," said Linda.

"And you sure don't make it easy. All right, listen," said Steffie with mock sternness, "Let's put it to a real test. You know the church bake sale and competition coming up? If you enter and do well, will that convince you that you can bake?"

"Ah, so that's the real reason you wanted me to join the church again, so you could embarrass me at the bake-off! I get it now."

"Oh, right. I would do that," said Steffie, hand on hip.

"You know I'm just kidding. But, seriously, isn't it pretty certain Granny Martha will win anyway? She always does."

"Oh, for Pete's sake … So what if she does? That's not really the point, is it?" argued Steffie, finally becoming exasperated.

Linda thought about it. She did enjoy the creative process, varying the recipes and sometimes using offbeat ingredients to add her own touches, and when they turned out well she felt good about it. She could enter the contest. She knew people wouldn't gag on her items; she was at least that good. She made a decision.

"Here's what I'm willing to do," she said. "I'll make two pear and almond tortes. You enter one of them under your name, and I'll enter the other one under my name. If you win, which you probably will because people know how good you are, then I'll be convinced I'm a baker. If I win, I'll have to start going to another church because the judges at this one must be crazy."

"It's a little deceitful, and may God forgive us, but okay it's a deal," said Steffie. "And if they pick the one with my name instead of yours, then we'll come clean. We'll admit you really baked them both."

79

"Fine," said Linda.

The next Sunday, as was their habit, Linda, Mae, and Linda's father went to church. As they settled into their pew, Linda looked up and noticed that Dan was in the choir. He gave her a nod of recognition, and she returned it. The service began, and Linda thought no more about it. She did notice the choir sounded unusually good. One pleasant baritone voice especially, unless it was just her imagination.

The sermon seemed long, although she had surreptitiously timed Pastor Frank's sermons more than once and found they rarely ran more than about 20 minutes. Usually they were pretty good too.

"Today we're in the Gospel of Matthew," Pastor Frank was saying, "in Chapter 16 where Jesus gets in the boat with His disciples and they're out on the lake and the disciples realize they have forgotten to bring lunch. Jesus says, 'Be on your guard against the leaven of the Pharisees,' and somehow the disciples think He is criticizing them for forgetting the bread.

"'No, that's not it!' Jesus says. 'And it's not even about the loaves and fishes thing we did before. I'm saying watch out for lies, hypocrisy, legalism, meaningless rituals, false teaching, customs and traditions masquerading as doctrine. They may sound good, but they're like bad yeast, growing and permeating everything until they are running your life. You find yourself listening to men instead of to God. Don't be fooled. Seek and stay close to God, and don't be afraid to stand up for the truth!'

"I can just imagine some of His disciples rolling their eyes," the pastor went on. "'We've just come from 'The Sermon on the Mount,' we're hungry, we don't have any bread, and now Jesus gives us 'The Sermon in the Boat.' What'll we do with Him? Next He'll be wanting us to walk on water!'"

Linda laughed with the rest of the congregation.

"And then Jesus might have reminded them," continued Pastor

Frank, "'While we were back there on the mountain I also said you who follow Me are the salt of the earth, but if the salt loses its saltiness it's no longer good for anything except to be thrown out and trampled.'

"And what did He mean by 'salt'? When God made you He didn't use a cookie cutter. Each of us is unique, and God has a plan for each of our lives. We have gifts, talents and passions that He gave us. We're 'salty' when we discover who we are and begin to live the life He intended for us instead of what the world expects. We're like dough in the oven, made with a very good recipe, and we're on the way to becoming something He's planned for us to be. Like the Israelites looking forward to the Promised Land, each of us has a destiny we need to move towards."

This is eerie, thought Linda.

"So for me, I want to be salty!" said Pastor Frank. "To paraphrase a former President, 'I am not a cookie!' And even if I were a cookie, I'd still want to be the best cookie I could be. With God's help, I'm going to stand tall in the life He wants for me.

"Now, in the words of Isaiah, 'Arise, shine, for your light has come, and the glory of the Lord rises upon you.' Let us pray."

Linda found herself praying silently all the way through the closing hymn, for guidance and direction, for her parents, for Steffie and the bakery, even for her ex-husband. And, more surprisingly, for Dan. This was a new thing.

She prayed about the bake-off too, not that she would win, but that she would at least do her best and not embarrass herself.

After the service it was customary to gather over coffee and juice in the fellowship hall. Linda usually just wanted to get home, but here came Dan, breaking himself out of a group of other choir members.

"Hi, Linda," he said, so softly Linda almost didn't hear him.

"Oh, hi, Dan," she answered.

81

"Nice sermon today, didn't you think?"

"Nice singing too," she said. "I didn't know you went to this church."

"Thank you. Steffie told me about the church. I'm new at the choir thing, but it's fun."

They both looked around nervously, avoiding eye contact, and then Linda said, "Oh, I'm sorry, let me introduce you to my parents. This is my mother, Mae, and this is my father. Mom and Dad, this is Dan. He comes into the Bread Box once in a while."

They all shook hands with "nice to meet you's."

"Look," said Dan, clearing his throat, "I'm sort of new in town and trying to get to know a few people, so I was wondering if I could take you all to lunch today, just to get acquainted."

"Sounds good to me," said Linda's father. "But I insist we go Dutch."

"Fair enough," said Dan.

"Hang on a minute now," said Mae, turning to Linda's father. "Don't you remember we have to get to Walmart today?"

"Walmart? I hate Walmart."

"You must have forgotten. A senior moment. Besides, I know you love looking at the fishing poles, or whatever. Linda can just go on with Dan, and we'll eat when we get home."

"Um, well okay," he said, studying his shoes.

A knowing look passed between Linda and Mae, and Linda was on her way out the side door with Dan in tow, though surprisingly she was not very hungry.

When they arrived at the pancake house in Dan's pickup, most of the after-church crowd was clearing out so they had no trouble getting a booth. They ordered, both choosing pancake and omelet combos as it turned out, which made Linda chuckle.

"Thanks for doing this," said Dan.

"Doing what?"

"Having lunch with a stranger."

"Apparently you can thank my mother. Anyway, you're a regular at the Bread Box, and Steffie seems to think you're okay."

"I apologize for that first day if I offended you somehow. Seemed like I might have."

"I wasn't offended," said Linda, "just puzzled maybe. But I got over it. Sorry if I was curt."

"I'm glad that's settled. It's been bothering me more than I expected for some reason."

"Me too, actually."

"So … tell me about Linda," Dan suggested.

Linda told him, but it was only stuff everybody else already knew about her. College, the divorce, leaving the bank and coming to work for Steffie. No secrets, no struggles, and no desires of the heart. It didn't take long, and she finished just as the food arrived.

"Now it's your turn," she said.

"But I'll have to talk with my mouth full."

"Just keep your food on your side of the table. To begin with, what are you doing here?"

"I make guitars."

"You make guitars."

"It's not so weird, is it?"

"I just never knew anyone who does that, is all. But I like guitar music. How did you get into that?"

"I got tired of being a stockbroker, even though I was fairly good at it. I had some money saved up, so I thought I'd take a sabbatical and get more involved in music, which is what I really love. I always have. I got out the guitar my parents gave me as a teenager to see if I could still play it, and I found I could."

"Like never forgetting how to ride a bicycle?" Linda offered.

"Yeah, but I was rusty and had to practice a lot to get it back."

"So you just quit work to play the guitar?"

"Well, no," Dan laughed. "I tried it out for a while first. I got into the worship band at my church, and I played some weekend coffee house gigs and put a few songs up on the Internet. It was fun, but after a while I just didn't feel I was cut out to be a full time performer.

"Then on a business trip to San Diego I took a tour of the Taylor Guitar factory near there and that's when I got the idea that maybe I could try my hand at making my own. I knew I'd never play guitar well enough to make a living at it, but I love the sound so much I thought it might be fun to see if I could make good guitars for others to play."

"That was quite a leap," said Linda.

"I already knew a little about woodworking. Carpentry's been kind of a hobby since I took Wood Shop in high school. Anyway, so that's when I quit the job and started working for a master luthier up near Asheville, as an apprentice."

"What's a luthier?" she asked. She said the word slowly, savoring the "th" sound and making Dan laugh.

"You're not developing a lisp, are you?" he said.

"Well no, but what *ith* it?"

That made him laugh some more.

"It'th … I mean *it's* a person who makes and repairs guitars and mandolins and such, but mostly guitars. The word comes from 'lute,' which was an early kind of guitar."

"So now you're a luthier too?"

"Trying to be. My first few attempts were laughable. Imagine a big cigar box with a cut off yard stick and some strings. Well, not that bad, but you get the idea."

Linda smiled.

"But finally the luthier said I had gotten good enough to go out on my own, so that's what I'm doing."

"Why here?"

"It's a small town, quiet, reasonable cost of living, not too far from the big city where my parents live, but still with opportunities for someone like me. No big chain stores selling instruments at cut rate prices, lots of people around who play music, and so on. I've got a few clients now, and I think it might work out. If not, I figure I'm still young enough to get back into something else."

"What about the women in your life?" Linda asked with some hesitation.

"You mean my mother and my sister?"

"No."

"Okay, well I guess I've been in love a few times, or thought I was. I was engaged once, but it kind of fell apart when I started my guitar phase. I think she was more in love with the successful stockbroker than with me, if you know what I mean."

Dan took a bite of pancake.

"I've made you talk, and you haven't eaten a thing. Eat!" she said.

As he did, Linda found herself wondering which it was that fascinated her more, the talk about making guitars or Dan himself. He was unique. And nice.

They lingered as their waitress kept returning with coffee refills. It felt … comfortable.

"So, you're happy you chose to come here?" she asked. "To this town, I mean, not the pancake house."

"Right," he said. "Yes, I am. Even more now that I've met you."

"And why is that?" she asked.

He answered, slowly. "Because now that we've broken the ice, I think you're very nice, and I like you."

"Well, thank you."

"And beautiful too," he said softly.

"What?"

"I said you're beautiful."

"Oh, right!"

"I mean it. You're are."

"Let's get out of here," said Linda. "The syrup must have gone to your brain!"

Dan laughed, and they got up, Dan paying on the way out. He drove Linda home without much more conversation. Walking her to the door of her parents' house, he said, "I really enjoyed this. Can we do it again?" She said yes.

Linda had never thought of herself as beautiful. Somewhat attractive maybe. She never had trouble getting dates in high school and college. As a result she was always being swept off her feet by a succession of boys with good looks and good lines. I married too young, she thought, before I really knew who I was, or who my husband was either. That's not going to happen again.

On the other hand, she was older now, wiser and more mature. And Dan's comments didn't sound like a line. He sounded like he meant it.

The weekend of the church baking contest was getting closer. Linda worked on perfecting her pear and almond torte but also found time to sit with Dan for a few minutes when he dropped in for his afternoon bear claw. Sometimes that meant staying later in the evening to tidy up the bookkeeping or review the latest advertisements proposed by the ad agency Steffie had hired. Often she suggested improvements, which pleased Steffie more than the agency people, but even they had to admit her ideas were good.

Matters with Dan quickly went beyond Sunday lunches at the pancake house. Linda looked forward to the evenings when they would have dinner somewhere or take in a concert at the college, or weekends and days off when they would go hiking or to a hootenanny in the state park with bluegrass music and barbecue. Sometimes Dan would bring a guitar and join in with one or two of the groups he knew. Linda would suggest an art gallery jaunt, and off they'd go. All the initial awkwardness was gone, and it felt good to be together.

Dan took her to visit his guitar shop a couple of times, in a converted garage behind his house just outside of town. It was fascinating even though she couldn't make head or tail out of what she was looking at, no matter how hard he tried to explain it.

One Monday morning as Linda came downstairs for breakfast Mae said, "Well, I guess you and Dan are an 'item' now, eh?"

"We're just good friends, Mom."

"You never were a very good liar, honey."

"Thanks, Mom."

"A mother knows these things."

"Whatever you say, Mom." Linda gulped her orange juice and headed for the door. "I'll get coffee and a Danish at the bakery."

"You'll be wearing those Danishes if you're not careful," said Mae, having the last word.

Linda had to admit Mae was right, but not about the Danishes.

Dan even went shopping with her a few times, when she needed help picking out something for Mae's birthday or finding decorations to make the Bread Box look more comfortable and inviting. Sometimes Linda would drive them in her Miata; sometimes they'd take the pickup. The puns were back too, including some real groaners, but they made her laugh.

But did Dan love Linda? He said he did. When they kissed and held each other, it seemed real enough. But was it? Something else to pray about.

Finally, the afternoon of the big Saturday church bake sale and competition came. Linda finished baking the tortes at the Bread Box in the morning. After a hurried lunch while they cooled, she and Steffie went to the church early to meet Dan and some other volunteers and help set up.

Back at the Bread Box, Steffie made an uncharacteristic fuss over which of Linda's identical tortes to enter under Linda's name and which would be attributed to Steffie.

"I don't care! Just pick one!" Linda fairly shouted at her in nervous frustration. Finally it was decided by a coin toss. The Saran Wrap was applied and off they went.

Dan had to leave before the judging in order to get to the city in time for dinner with his parents for their anniversary, so he missed all the fun, such as it was

The judges tried to make the process as dramatic as they could, but for Linda and Steffie it was excruciatingly tedious. The outcome was almost anticlimactic. Linda didn't win first prize, and neither did Steffie. Granny Martha won again, as usual. But coming in second wasn't so bad, especially since Steffie came in third with Linda's other torte. Linda and Steffie confessed, and Steffie disqualified herself for entering under false pretenses. That let the fourth place winner step into third place, which made everything kosher and everybody happy, especially since it was Pastor Frank's wife.

"I have to admit, this is very good," said Mae, enjoying a slice of pear and almond torte for dessert that evening.

"Thanks, Mom," said Linda, gathering up the dishes.

"Me too!" said her father.

Linda enjoyed the few moments alone that came with doing dishes. As she rinsed them, loaded the dishwasher, scrubbed a pot or a frying pan, and generally tidied up, she had time to reflect.

She hadn't yet told her parents that Steffie had asked her a few weeks ago, before the bake-off, to think about becoming a partner in the bakery. It would mean making a sizeable investment, and she wasn't sure how Mae would react. On the other hand, she wasn't sure if it really made any difference what Mae thought, although it would be nice if she and her father approved.

And it hadn't taken the bake-off to tell her she had become good at baking. She already knew. Brownies aren't the secret of life, she knew, but wasn't it she herself who had started with Mae's recipes and Steffie's hints and encouragement and created something that was hers alone?

It's about leaven and salt, she thought to herself. What's in the recipes, and maybe more important, what's in me. Praying about it hadn't hurt either.

The phone rang.

"It's Dan, for you," said Mae, bringing the phone into the kitchen.

"I'm sorry I couldn't stay for the judging," Dan said, over highway noise in the background. "What happened?"

Linda told him.

"Congratulations! Can I take you out someplace to celebrate?"

"Give me ten minutes to get ready."

It was a warm evening, but Dan insisted on the truck instead of the top down Miata. They drove out of town and onto a narrow road that eventually began to climb, winding through shadowed woods and past moonlit meadows, until they reached the crest of a ridge. They parked where a break in the trees formed a natural overlook. Spread out before them was the town and surrounding countryside, bathed in the light of a full moon.

"Where are we?" asked Linda.

"I think you know," said Dan with a mischievous grin. "I'm told it's the local lovers' lane."

"Well, yes, now that you mention it, maybe I have been here a time or two," she admitted.

"I had a really fun time trying to figure out how to get here, including a 'dry run' in the rain last week. This place ain't on my GPS!"

They got out of the truck and stood hand in hand gazing down at the view. Dan moved closer and put his arm around her waist. "It's a nice view, isn't it?" he said quietly.

"Yes, it is," she answered. "I've always liked it. In fact I usually liked the view better than the company."

"What about tonight?" Dan said.

"Tonight is … different," she was surprised to hear herself say. "I think I like the company better this time."

"I know I sure do," said Dan.

"And I thought you brought me all the way up here just to congratulate me on my baking skills." Linda still wondered what it was that had attracted Dan to her. Surely not something as shallow as that.

As if reading her mind, Dan said, "It was never the baking."

He turned to face her, his own face almost silhouetted in the moonlight.

"Oh sure, the brownies were great, but I noticed you were determined to try other stuff as well, and then you decided you really liked baking. Ever since Steffie offered you a part ownership you've been thinking it through very carefully. There was a time when you probably would have turned it down right away. You haven't said so, but I think you've decided you can handle it and you want to do it. That you're good enough."

"Wow," said Linda. "It's like you're reading my mind, Dan."

"You're a person who knows who she is, and I mean way beyond just baking. Maybe you didn't always know, but now you do. I hope this doesn't sound stupid, but you've torn down some walls you'd built up. You're trusting yourself more now, not afraid to test yourself and grow and then lead from your strengths and step out and become the you who's always been in there. And I like who you are. No, I love who you are."

It didn't sound stupid to Linda at all. It sounded good, very good.

"And by the way, I still think you're beautiful. More beautiful all the time. So I don't just love the baker. I love Linda." Then Dan stopped talking.

Linda was silent for a long time. Then, and for the first time, she said, "I love you too, Dan."

It was Dan's turn to say, "Wow." He put his arms around her and they kissed.

"But it's not as easy as all that," Linda continued, backing away a little. "I don't have the money to invest in the bakery. I know I can probably get a loan from the bank, but I used to work in a bank and I know what's involved. It's a big deal."

"I know it is, but I also know you'll be okay with it."

"I just wish I could be sure," she said.

"I think you *are* sure. And anyway, I can lend you the money myself."

"No, I need to do this on my own."

"If we were married, then half my stuff would be yours. It would be your money."

"Is that a proposal?" said Linda.

Dan got down on one knee and took her hand. "Yes, it is. Linda, will you marry me?"

Linda looked at him for a long moment before saying, "Yes, Dan, I will."

He stood up and kissed her again.

"Thank you," he said. "You may not believe it, but I've been praying about this for a long time. And I've been carrying *this* around for about a month."

Dan opened a small black box and slipped a diamond ring on her finger.

"I hope it fits," he said.

"It's perfect."

"I don't know about you, but I've gained six pounds since I met you. And I have uneaten bear claws stacked to the rafters in my house."

"I'm not telling you how much *I* weigh," said Linda.

"On you it looks good."

"Are you still sure you're not just marrying me for my brownies?" she countered.

"Are you still sure you're not just marrying me for my money?"

"I hope you know better than that," she said.

Linda pulled him into her arms and they kissed again, for a long, long time.

Bridges

He is a shell incomplete,
lacking true love to make him feel whole.
She dwells in innocence sweet,
looking not for a lover to shelter her soul.
And they're drifting along, and the river flows.

Love is a force with a mind of its own.
Though patient and kind, it won't be overthrown.
It can build a bridge without iron or stone while the river flows.

Two hearts with one destiny,
as a new start and bright road appear,
when love's call of sweet mystery
spans the heavens to cancel both distance and fear.
And they're walking as one where the river flows.

Love is a force with a mind of its own.
Though patient and kind, it won't be overthrown.
It can build a bridge without iron or stone while the river flows.

Never Moor

Look how the wind sweeps across to the sea
as it bears you forever e'er farther from me.
Grass turning amber like old sheaves of grain;
aye, the moor mocks me gently to add to my pain,
for I know in my heart nevermore will there be
aught but bittersweet sorrow you've set yourself free.

Gone and no reason, no recourse to save.
Off to find you a new world, a new road to pave.
No more the comfort we shared as of old;
now my hope's rendered brittle; it shatters with cold.
As the Sun dimly sets behind clouds dark with rain
fading dreams are the last place I'll see you again.

Family Tree Leaves
A bluegrass favorite

I have a son-in-law whose mother was a big genealogy fan. She loved to do research into people's family trees. She was happy enough when her son married my daughter, but when I told her a little about *our* family tree not long after that, she got real quiet. Here's what I told her.

My Grandpa was a mailman when stamps were three cents each.
He couldn't read addresses right so they took him off the streets.
Promoted him to management, a cushy job downtown,
but he couldn't find his office, and he just walked 'round and 'round.

My daddy was a lineman in Kentucky 'fore the War.
Made a circuit of the county climbing poles to check the power.
He never feared the danger posed by live wires in a storm,
but he got too close and now he's toast. You might say he got transformed.

Chorus
My family tree leaves a lot to be desired.
My great grandpa was not too pleased with the progeny he sired.
Each offspring's life experience worse than the one before.
It's got short branches on its trunk. Its roots in shifting sands are sunk.
This tree has borne no fruit … but it's got nuts galore!

My uncle, he was self-employed. Recycling was his game,
collecting cans and bottles for deposits and spare change.
Along the roads and highways my green uncle could be seen,
until a speeding hybrid car caused him to be redeemed.

And as for me, my history's no better than the rest.
I'm writing songs that no one sings, and often I'm depressed.
A hippie in September years remembering what was,
and living on prescription drugs that don't give me a buzz.

(Repeat Chorus)

But wait …
My son, well he's a lawyer, and before you start to laugh,
he does it all *pro bono* with a dedicated staff.
He's helping other people worse off than you and me.
So finally something good has sprung from my nutty family tree.

Yeah, finally something good has sprung from my nutty family tree.

Day of the Science Fiction Thing

Eat your heart out, Orson Scott Card!

Blanket Coverage

(An earlier version of this story originally appeared
in the first issue of *Galileo Magazine,* September 1976.)

Houston, September 7 (UP). NASA confirmed today that America's first husband and wife astronaut team is lost in space. The announcement came after video transmissions from the space shuttle Sunbeam ended abruptly Tuesday night as an estimated 20 million viewers watched.

The astronauts, Air Force Lt Colonel Ralph Polo, 34, and his wife Margo, 31, a biologist, were launched Labor Day morning on a controversial mission to test the effects of space conditions on human reproduction.

Col and Mrs Polo were preparing to dock with the International Space Station when the Sunbeam vanished from radar and stopped sending telemetry. Officials refused to comment on speculation the disappearance is related to recent UFO sightings.

Congressman J Hooper Harper (D-SC), a longtime critic of the space program, demanded a full investigation. "It was bad enough spending millions on a worthless mission to satisfy some scientists' prurient interests, but now to have those two young folks lost in space, why it's unconscionable," he said.

The White House is expected to issue a statement tomorrow.

* * *

You know those times when everything seems to hit the fan at once? I hadn't even gotten all my Christmas bills paid, and now it looked like the old TV in our bedroom was about to die. That, plus new tires and repairs to the furnace, was putting my modest salary as Larry Walden, public relations guy for Statewise Insurance Company, to the test.

I must have said something out loud about the TV, probably a good four letters worth, because my wife, Amy, half asleep as she usually is when we watch TV in bed, shifted a little and mumbled something unintelligible.

"Click," went the thermostat control for her half of the electric blanket. She had most of my half of the blanket on her side of the bed. My half wasn't turned on. If one control clicks whenever it goes on or off, imagine what two of them sound like. All night long, "click, click, clickety-click." I can't doze off with all that racket, so I lie in the cold and let the TV bore me to sleep. Which is a shame, since the blanket was expensive. My Christmas present to Amy.

Admittedly sort of a selfish gift since the blanket covers the whole bed and has dual controls. But, as you see, she does get most of the use of it. I get "Sermonette" and not one, but two sets of Ginsu knives for $19.95. So it's truly better to give than to receive.

Anyway, there I was, witnessing the demise of my picture tube and getting madder by the minute as it displayed nothing but a shimmering of strange, indistinct shapes.

I didn't give the TV any thought at work the next day. It's hard for your domestic life to intrude when you're absorbed in the exciting activities that go with a job like mine. I spent the morning tracking down a shipment of uniforms for the Statewise Insurance Little League team. I had lunch with a magazine writer who wanted to know whether men or women have more accidents while texting, and in the afternoon I entertained two busloads of visiting Japanese claims adjustors (one bus for them and one for their cameras). With all that, it's no wonder the company's annual report, which I also produce, looks like something from Junior Achievement.

But, almost before I knew it, I was home again watching TV and listening to the electric blanket. That's when I noticed the relationship between them for the first time. Or thought I did.

"Click," went Amy's control. Screwy went the picture.

With the curiosity of an engineer, if not the training (industrial psychology is my game), I felt under Amy's side of the blanket to see whether the click meant it was on or off. It was on. I might have felt around a little more just for fun, but then it clicked again, and when I looked back at the TV the picture was fine. It was explaining the virtues of a reverse mortgage.

I reached over and nudged the control knob higher until it clicked on again. Sure enough, the picture squiggled. That was good! It meant the trouble was with the blanket, and I wouldn't have to replace the TV. And the blanket was still under warranty.

By that time, I was curious enough to do some more experimenting. When Amy's control clicked off, I clicked mine on, and the picture squiggled. Then, the supreme test: Keeping an eye on my control in case it clicked off, I stealthily reached over and turned Amy's control on.

Well, the picture went crazy. There was something odd about the way it went crazy, though. It was not a random craziness, like you would expect from simple electrical interference. It was patterns, sort of, and they didn't move around much. I shoved both controls up to their highest positions so they wouldn't click off, and I watched those fuzzy patterns. There was something about them.

Of course, wrapped up in my patterns as I was, it didn't dawn on me that my wife was being roasted alive. She let me know about it. I can't remember the last time I saw her that awake after 11:00 on a week night.

"Would you mind telling me why I have awakened in a sauna to the sight of my husband with his eyes glued to a test pattern, or is this a dream?" she said icily. Get it – icily?

"Look at the TV," I said, snatching her control out of her reach.

"Why? Come on, it's hot under here, Larry!" she said.

"But look at it," I said.

"It's a test pattern. Which means it's very late. Please!"

"That is not a test pattern," I said. "It's more like … geometry … or hieroglyphics, maybe."

Amy didn't say anything then, and I could see she was looking at the screen with some interest.

"The electric blanket is doing that," I said.

"The blanket?" she shrilled.

I nodded. She jumped out of bed and unplugged the blanket, hard, by the wires.

"Hey! What was that for?" Behind a very big gun, Clint Eastwood looked sternly in our direction.

"It's bad enough having a husband who watches test patterns in the middle of the night," Amy said firmly, "but I draw the line at sleeping under a defective electric blanket."

Her body language told me she meant it. The only thing to do was take the blanket off, fold it up, and put it under the nightstand until I could take it back to the store. After that, we both stood there for a minute contemplating our naked bed.

"You know," I mumbled, "now there's only one good way to keep warm …"

I'm glad she wasn't really mad.

I remembered to throw the blanket and the sales receipt in the back seat as I left for work the next morning, so the previous night's TV viewing was more or less on my mind when I got to the office. The first event was a meeting on how to tell one of our high profile clients we were going to have to deny a big claim, while minimizing media attention. As usual, the first ten minutes in the conference room consisted of small talk while those who had arrived on time waited for those who hadn't. I casually mentioned my experience with the blanket to Jerry Whitehead.

Jerry is our senior technical underwriter as well as an old fraternity brother. In fact, he got me my job with Statewise after I'd tried the New York PR agency bit for a while and decided the big city suck-up routine wasn't for me.

His interest was surprisingly serious for a subject I only considered worthy of idle conversation. I didn't realize just how serious until after the meeting when he asked me to drop up to his office. There he made me repeat the story, which I did, while he sat looking pensive. When I finished, he was silent for a few seconds before asking, "What brand of blanket is it?"

I told him. A Sunbeam. Deluxe king size.

Then he said something I didn't expect. "The same thing happened at my house."

It was my turn to be silent, although I admit I was thinking, Okay, so there's a batch of defective blankets out there. The Sunbeam PR man has an unpleasant meeting in his future.

"It also happened to two other people I know," he continued. "All Sunbeams. Their blankets, I mean. Larry, there's something funny peculiar about this."

"About a bunch of defective electric blankets?"

"No, about the patterns on the television screens mostly." He paused. "Did you say you have your blanket out in the car?"

"Yeah …"

"Could you bring it in here? I'd like to run some tests over in the lab with it, if you don't mind."

"Listen, Jerry, after the client finds out we're denying this claim,

I'm going to have the Bluetooth in my ear all afternoon pacifying the trade press and the stockbrokers, so I've got to go and get ready now. Somehow, I don't think the Great Electric Blanket Mystery is a job for good ole Lawrence of Public Relations."

But what the heck, I owed him. So I got the blanket. What was really on my mind was whether Jerry would tamper with it and obviate the warranty, but he promised he wouldn't.

My afternoon was a disaster, as expected, and besides that, Jerry said the blanket trick didn't work in the lab for some reason and could he come over after dinner that night and try it out on my bed. Nothing beats actual field conditions for scientific experiments, I guess. I don't remember what I told Amy to placate her, but we hadn't seen the Whiteheads socially for a while, and Jerry promised to bring his wife, Janet, over with him.

The evening started out reasonably well. Then around nine we all went to the bedroom to play with the blanket. Amy wore a forced smile, probably wondering what our neighbors would think, but our curiosity was aroused, so we helped Jerry spread the blanket on the bed. I plugged it in, set the controls and turned on the TV.

The fuzzy patterns were there again, just like before. I wondered what Jerry's engineer mind would make of it.

"Well, what do you make of it?" he said.

"No fair!" I said. "You're the expert!"

The girls chuckled a little – stage chuckles.

"Your symbols are just like mine, Larry." He called them symbols. "These same symbols appear on our TV screen at home when I turn on our blanket, and they're the same as the symbols the other people have told me about."

"Look, Jerry," I said, "I'm not going to be a very good Dr Watson for you. The last time I saw a strange electronic phenomenon was when a friend in high school stuck his guitar amplifier jack into his mouth and got the local radio station. That was weird enough for me."

"Wow, you're really taking this personally," said Janet, laughing.

"Listen, I can bob my Adam's apple up and down, cross my eyes, curl my tongue, and lean forward at a 75 degree angle without falling down, all at the same time, but I am absolutely not technical."

"Okay, okay," said Jerry indulgently. "I get the message. I guess it *is* getting a little late."

"No, I don't mean to throw you out. It's just that, whatever this is about, you need to tell me straight, because there's no way I'm going to figure it out by myself."

"Fair enough. In that case, may I come over again tomorrow night with some other people and run some real experiments?"

"Is there any reason you can't do it at your house?"

"Well, your blanket is a king size. Ours is only a double, and it doesn't make as clear an image on the TV."

Amy coughed, but I don't think she had a cold.

"So you have a theory about all this?" I asked.

"Yes," said Jerry. "I think the symbols are a message of some kind."

"Oh, yeah, right!" I said. "And it probably says, 'Help, I'm a prisoner in an electric blanket factory!'"

Work the next day took my mind off blankets, but I did do some thinking as I drove home. True, I'm not technical, but anybody with a high school education knows a little about how radio transmitters work. Run a current through a wire and the wire gives off electromagnetic radiation. If you take a wire and short circuit a flashlight battery near a radio, you'll get static, especially if it's on the AM band. You've made a crude radio transmitter, sending signals by repeated circuit breaking. The only difference is that a regular radio transmitter controls the energy to make intelligible signals when "decoded" in the receiver.

Since an electric blanket is basically a network of wires with electricity going through them, why shouldn't it act like a radio transmitter? Or in this case a TV transmitter, which amounted to the same thing.

But why did all the blankets transmit the same patterns, or symbols, or whatever they were?

Well, no doubt Jerry already had it figured out. I was content to wait until he explained it to me, but the whole business was getting to be a pain. Not being able to relax at home after a hard day is no fun. And poor Amy, cleaning the house from top to bottom two days in a row for company. She didn't really have to, of course, but I appreciated it just the same.

Still, nothing prepared me for the sight that greeted me when the doorbell rang after dinner. Jerry and Janet were there with their blanket, as expected, but behind them was a crowd of strangers, including a uniformed policeman. The street was full of parked cars. Before I could react in terror like any normal person, I noticed the policeman was also carrying a blanket.

Jerry sensed my apprehension, and I could see he was a little embarrassed. "Sorry I didn't warn you a little better, Larry …"

"You didn't warn me at all!"

"Yeah, well, I am sorry. Look, I think we're really onto something here, and these people have agreed to help us figure it out."

"You mean help *you* figure it out!"

"Larry and Amy, I want you to meet some people," said Jerry. "This is Officer Lou Smith, a neighbor of mine."

"Hi," said the policeman, extending his right hand from under his blanket, which was baby pink. The blanket, I mean. "It's okay; I'm off duty."

"That's a relief," I said, but I'm not sure I meant it. I'm always self-conscious around policemen.

"This is Ralph Proczak," said Jerry, "the other guy I mentioned whose blanket acts like ours."

Proczak had a blue blanket. We shook hands.

"And these gentlemen are Rev. Tom Kinder, up from Texas, and Allen Mercer and Dr Ralph Corelli, who are with the government."

"Which government?" I asked.

"Very funny," said Jerry.

"Okay, but where are their blankets?" Mercer had a fancy digital camera, but that was all.

"Allen is a cryptographer, and Dr Corelli is an astronomer." As if that explained everything.

Like I said, I think Jerry already had it figured out. His selection of friends seemed carefully designed to prove *some* theory or other.

"Well, come on in everybody," I said gamely. "Jerry can lead us to the bedroom."

What a weird thing to be saying to this bunch. And what do you serve a group like this? I looked at Amy, hoping she would think of something. She got the message and rolling her eyes headed to the kitchen. Janet followed.

Somehow, the rest of us squeezed into the bedroom while I tried to remember how much beer we had.

As if it were his own house, Jerry calmly began placing the electric blankets on the bed and plugging them in. There were four, including mine. I attempted some small talk.

"So, Mr ... uh, Mercer, I always thought a cryptographer was somebody who takes pictures of tombstones."

"Jerry, your friend really is very funny," said Mercer.

"You have to say that. It's his house," said Jerry.

Finally everything was set up, and Jerry had the TV on to a Star Trek re-run. He muted the sound and then spoke to us like a science teacher.

"Gentlemen," he started, "here is what we know and what we don't know. Sunbeam electric blankets, and only Sunbeams by the way, cause symbols to appear on TV screens. It doesn't matter if the TV is a flat screen or has a tube or whether it's on cable or antenna. Turning on both halves of the blanket makes a stronger image than just using one half, and a king size blanket works better than a double. So far, it's been impossible to make out what the symbols are. Hypothesis: The signals are still too weak, and the more blankets we use, the more the signals will be amplified."

"Wait a minute," I said. "I bet you also know the ignition temperature of cotton bed sheets. How many electric blankets does it take before we all go up in smoke?"

"Another thing we know," said Jerry, ignoring me, "is that this only works at night. Now if the blankets were doing this all by themselves, the phenomenon should be visible at all times. Hypothesis: The blankets are receiving signals from another source, one that's active only at night, and they are retransmitting them to the television receiver."

"A minor correction, Mr Whitehead," interrupted Corelli, the astronomer. "The source of transmissions may be active only at night, as you said, or it may be that we are in a physical position to *receive* only at night."

"It sounds like you're suggesting the transmissions may be of extraterrestrial origin," said Rev. Kinder.

"That's exactly right," said Jerry to nobody's apparent astonishment but mine, and maybe Officer Smith's. "I think they are coming from outer space and we're lined up properly with them only during certain hours at night. Due to the Earth's rotation, we're facing away from the source in the daytime. Now, what we don't know is the source and what meaning, if any, the symbols may have."

It doesn't always pay to second guess a senior technical underwriter with an engineering degree, but I couldn't stop trying to figure out the mystery in light of the cast of characters Jerry had assembled. I suppose there were several things an engineer, a cryptographer, an astronomer, and a minister could have added up to, but I blurted out the first thing that came into my head.

"You mean to tell me you think God is speaking to us through Sunbeam electric blankets?"

They all laughed at that, although I noticed Proczak and Smith were laughing less than the others. I didn't know whether the idea was a laughing matter or not. I guess it would depend on what God was saying to us, right? And at that point we didn't know what that was.

"As exciting as that prospect would be, Mr Walden," said Rev. Kinder in an oil-upon-the-waters voice, "I suspect what we have here is far more mundane."

"I would have thought 'mundane' and 'extraterrestrial' were mutually exclusive concepts when applied to the same phenomenon," offered Proczak.

"Oh, I guess I forgot to mention Dr Proczak is a professor of philosophy at the University," explained Jerry.

"I hope what we learn tonight will explain this apparent paradox, Dr Proczak," said Rev. Kinder.

I was with Proczak all the way.

"Okay, now let's get down to business," said Jerry. "I'm going to turn on all the blankets and then find an empty TV channel, and we'll see what we get."

"Clickety-clickety-click-click-click," went the controls on the blankets as Jerry turned them all the way up. I could almost see little shimmering heat waves rising from the bed. Mercer got his camera ready. Jerry flipped the TV remote a couple of times until he found a channel he liked. Then he stepped back so everybody could see the screen.

We all gasped in unison. This time the image was very clear. There was no mistaking it. And it was in English!

"Pizza rolls, everybody!" announced Amy, bouncing in from the kitchen with Janet close behind.

"Wow! Is it ever hot in here!" said Janet. "What are you guys doing?"

The timing was terrible, but it broke the spell and brought us all down to Earth, so to speak.

When nobody said anything, Amy and Janet finally got the idea we weren't in a playful mood. Then they saw the TV screen.

HELLO HOUSTON
A-OK & WISH YOU WERE HERE
ALSO WISH PICKLES & ICE CREAM
MESSAGES EVERY 10 DAYS
POLOS

"Jerry, you don't look as surprised as the rest of us," I said, breaking the silence.

Mercer started taking pictures of the screen with his camera. Amy put the pizza rolls down on the bed, where they'd keep warm.

"No," said Jerry, "but I'm still amazed by it. I'm not sure exactly what made me suspect this was about the missing astronauts—too many coincidences, I guess—but I did think that's what it was. Actually, Mr Mercer and Dr Corelli here are from NASA. Rev. Kinder is the Polos' pastor, the one who married them, in fact, just before they went on their mission."

"I have a feeling there is something you've been holding back from your PR Department, Jerry, my friend," I said.

Jerry laughed. "I'm afraid so," he said. "You know we do get secret contracts occasionally. I can't even tell Janet about them. We've insured the space shuttles ever since Boeing dropped Lloyd's of London in order to 'buy American,' and so we've been trying to solve the astronauts' disappearance almost since the day it took place. We were getting nowhere until the electric blankets started acting up."

About that time, I noticed Proczak the philosopher had fainted. Janet tried to revive him while Rev. Kinder repeated "pickles and ice cream" over and over with a silly grin on his face. Mercer and Corelli whipped out their cell phones, I guess to call NASA in Houston.

By now you know the rest, since it's been in the news *ad nauseum,* along with all the new UFO sightings. Based on subsequent reports from the Polos, NASA says aliens came along looking for zoo specimens. Their arrival coincided with the Polos' flight, and it was a perfect opportunity to grab a matched pair of humans. It's caused quite a stir among us earthlings, but at least it's displaced a lot of stories about government scandals, war and crime and the economy, which is no doubt a very good side effect.

The Polos have a Sunbeam electric baby blanket that operates on solar power from whatever sun they're near. They have it "tuned" to our Sunbeam blankets, and somehow that lets them send their messages. How they can do it from light years away and without the aliens knowing is a mystery to me, but maybe the aliens do know and the Polos just don't know they know, you know?

The Polos say they'll be returned in two years, and they're okay with that. After all, what astronaut wouldn't pass up a chance like this? Unless the aliens decide to eat them. But nobody seems too worried about it. I hope they bring back pictures. And tee shirts.

As for me, I bought three more Sunbeam electric blankets, with quieter controls of course, so Amy and I would have front row seats for all the new messages. Also, I got a hefty raise for the way I've handled the PR on this. So while I'm still just your friendly neighborhood public relations guy for Statewise Insurance, Amy and I now have a nice new, and very large, flat screen TV.

And lately Amy has developed a taste for pickles and ice cream.

111

Lament of the Expectant Parent

Apparently I'm going to be
a parent.
Lament, lament, lament.
I'd rather just go stick
my head in
cement, cement, cement.

The Meeting at the Center of the Universe

(Originally published in *Fusion*, a sci-fi anthology of winners
of the Fantastic Books International Charity
Short Story Competition, 2012)

Nobody is sure where the idea came from, but it was clearly time for a summit meeting of all civilizations.

The call went out on a Friday, and planning began immediately. That is, it was a Friday on Earth, but that didn't really matter since the Earth calendar had long since been adopted as universal, modified locally only as necessary to accommodate differences in planetary rotation cycles and speeds of circumnavigation around suns in all the various worlds where it applied. So it was Universal Friday.

Most civilizations had the technology to traverse multiple-light-year distances in anywhere from instantaneously to no more than a day or two. Some had star drives, some had harnessed wormholes or could create and use them at will, and some could project themselves and their luggage holographically over great distances and then use local atomic material at the destination to reconstitute themselves on the spot as tangible objects or beings who maintained instantaneous communication with their "originals" back home. Others had learned how to magnify greatly the effects of transporter technology originally developed for relatively short distances. Civilizations who hadn't achieved star travel were encouraged to hitch rides with those who had. The call invited even those worlds who had so far remained hidden and unknown, whether by choice or by oversight, to come join the convocation.

It would be the first annual summit meeting of all the vast multitudes of federations, leagues, empires, coalitions, republics, kingdoms, dictatorships, hegemonies, solar systems, and planets, both natural and artificial.

Of course, there was only one place that made sense for the meeting to be held – The Center of the Universe. That way, no favoritism would be shown by holding it close to this civilization or to that one. And no one would be more or less inconvenienced by the distance than anyone else, although distance hardly mattered to most.

Such a crowd would require a large venue, even if each delegation was limited to three representatives, two transformation engineers, and a small retinue. The Universe is big—infinite in fact—so surely such a place could be found almost anywhere, and especially at the center. Unless the center was a black hole. But nobody believed it was. That was just an ancient 21st Century superstition.

Upon arrival, the delegations would identify a suitable venue close enough to be declared the center for all practical purposes, and the engineers would quickly create and outfit a facility using conventional energy/matter transformation devices.

The first annual Universal Summit Meeting was now just three weeks away. A short time to prepare, but given the urgency of the agenda, the timing was justified.

Among the agenda items:
1. Stabilization of exchange rates between the Ʉni and local currencies
2. Amnesty for third world aliens
3. Legalization of marijuana for medical purposes
4. Universal warming

Feverish preparations. Urgent messages back and forth. Hurried consultations. Agreements on protocol. Intense studying of the issues by the delegates, last minute instructions from their governments, and fine tuning of diplomacy training for retinue staff.

Relentlessly, the day for departure approached. Starships were outfitted. Wormhole calibrations were tweaked. Universal language translators were updated. Projectors and transporters were tested and re-tested, with new and redundant parts installed in fail-safe systems. Rendezvous arrangements were made.

A Universal Thursday was the agreed departure date for everyone to begin the journey from home worlds to the Summit venue.

Universal Sunday was to be the big welcoming banquet, followed on Monday by a brief opening plenary session. The remainder of the week would see a full schedule of committee meetings, subcommittee meetings, workshops, presentations of papers, debates, writing and submission of resolutions and motions, and communication back to the home worlds for reaction and further instructions, all culminating in a second plenary session on Saturday for formal arguments. The next Universal Sunday would be a day of rest and recreation, maybe time for some sightseeing at the Center of the Universe, and then on Monday final preparations would be made for voting in the closing plenary session on Tuesday. Almost two Universal Weeks in all.

Finally, it was time to go. The travelers entered their ships or mounted their pads or stood before their star gates.

The simple command was given. "Take us to the Center!"

And nothing happened.

Anxious moments. Angry stares. Frenzied double and triple checking of equipment. Calls going from civilization to civilization: "What's going on?" "We'll be late; don't start without us!" "What, are you stuck too?"

Until somebody—a seminary student in a backwater solar system at the edge of one of the smaller galaxies—realized the truth: If the Universe is infinite, then every point is the center. And that means everybody was already there. At the Center of the Universe.

Next year's meeting will be held on Rigel IV.

Alien for Dinner

Or how an hors d'oeuvre saved the Earth

I dreamed the alien showed up at dinnertime,
all tentacles and smiles and get-to-know-ya.
Three-fingered hands reached out in eager pantomime
while grave suspicions fed my paranoia.

I'm more than glad to represent Earth's race
to visitors who land from outer space,
but too much glee when hastening to greet me
spelled a less than diplomatic plan to eat me.

There has to be a better way, I signed,
than eating hosts wherever you alight.
There's better food I'll try my best to find
before my head becomes a tasty bite.

Reacting fast I offered cheese and crackers
which was all I had on hand to buy some time,
but it satisfied a need, and my attacker's
hungry drool turned into happy slime.

A grin appearing in a gaping orifice?
A mundane snack averting mankind's end?
What caused this quite surprising metamorphosis
from predator to everlasting friend?

For every nationality or strangest galaxality,
no matter color, size and shape or name,
shown love and hospitality it's simply a reality:
beneath the carapace we're all the same.

When Superheroes Learn to Fly, Part 1: The Fledgling S

Thump, thump, thump, thump, thump … Flomp!
Ow!
   C'mon, Clark, you can do it!
Why do I have to fly? Why can't I just be like other boys?
   First time you hit a baseball, we never found it.
Anyway, look, I can already jump over the barn.
… *WHUMP!*
See? In a single bound.
And I can beat a bullet. Ka-Pow!
   What you need is a leap of faith, Son. Believe you can fly.

Why? I'm not a bird, or a plane. Look, up in the sky—forget it!
Besides, I'm afraid of heights.
   Everyone is afraid of heights at first. You'll get over it.

Why can't I just be strong, say like a locomotive? You know I'm
strong!
Why can't I just try out for high jumping in the Olympics? You know
I'd win.
   No, no, no, no, no … We can't let people know about your powers.
Not even Lois?
   Not yet.

Lois and Lex would laugh at me anyway.
But they don't know I can see their underwear.
   Hey, what did we tell you about that?
Aww!
   Never mind them. Remember: Truth, justice and the American way.
   You'll understand someday, and so will they.

You're not my real parents anyway.

Why do you say that?

You said you found me in the cornfield. That's crazy. Pete says his folks found him under a cabbage leaf, and he's 11 so he knows stuff.

We don't grow any cabbage here.

It's not fair! Even Jesus couldn't fly.

No, but He walked on water.

I bet that was easier.

You watch your tongue, boy.

Thump, thump, thump, thump, thump … Flomp!
Ow!!

Oh, Jonathan, he's frightening the chickens!

See, Pa, they can't hardly fly either. This is dumb!

Clark, Clark, Clark, Clark, Clark! Try again.

Not even Gladiator or The Phantom, or Mandrake the Magician. They can't fly.

Even Flash Gordon needs a rocket ship, Pa.

Once more, Clark, just one more time. Please?

Thump, thump, thump, thump, thump … Flomp!
OW!!!

Oh, all right, let's call it a day.

Yay!

We'll try again tomorrow.

Awww!!

The Prophecy Booth

"The farther back you can look, the
farther forward you are likely to see."
– Winston Churchill during WWII

They called it Area 61. Blackout curtains covered the windows. Computer screens displayed images I couldn't decipher. Wires ran everywhere. There was a faint, low-pitched hum.

In the center was a swivel chair between two thick Erector Set-like columns bridged at the top like a crude airport security screening machine. A red bicycle helmet hung from overhead, its inside bristling with electrodes.

The set up looked like a sporty electric chair but without the arm and leg restraints.

"Would *monsieur* care to take a seat?" asked Ed with a grand gesture.

I sat. Ed put the helmet on my head. He fingered what looked like a TV remote and the humming noise got louder, then subsided.

I blinked.

Suddenly I saw two views of the room, one superimposed on the other. There were two Anitas, one seated at a computer looking at the screen and the other looking at me. There were two of everyone. Somebody knocked on the door. Judy, Juan and Mike looked up but also continued to look at their computer screens. One of the Anitas opened the door and the kid who picks up the mail stepped into the room, handed her a large manila envelope, and left. Then everything went back to normal. That is, to where there was only one of each person.

"Okay," said Ed, "now let's just sit tight for a minute."

Somebody knocked on the door. Judy, Juan and Mike looked up. Anita opened the door and the kid who picks up the mail stepped into the room, handed her a large manila envelope, and left.

ONE

You never can tell what's going to happen in a brainstorming session, and certainly no one would have predicted what came from this one. I had arrived, predictably late, just as our CEO, Jack Gamble, was saying, "If we can see into the past, why can't we see into the future?"

Jack glanced up at me from the antique captain's chair he favors as his "perch of honor" in these sessions. "Anita, why don't you fill Art in? I'll go get a refill on this coffee."

"Well, I'm not sure where to start." Anita Rondo has a Ph.D. in applied mathematics and is the leader of our product development group, a team of level headed techies who know how to think outside the box, but with discipline, fully understanding the need to be practical. "Maybe you should just look at this first. Jack brought it in."

She handed me a local business magazine, opened to an article about anticipating changes in the business environment.

"I've read dozens of these," I said. "What's the big deal with this one?"

"No big deal about that one, Art," answered Jack, settling back into his chair, a full mug of coffee in hand. "And that's just it. For all the talk about anticipating change, the one thing that hasn't changed in probably 50 years is all the talk about anticipating change."

"I know I certainly anticipate change whenever I hand a clerk a five dollar bill for a three-fifty purchase!"

That brought groans from around the table.

"Edward!" said Anita, rolling her eyes, "We're trying to be serious here."

"Yeah, Ed, why can't *you* change?" said somebody from the far end of the table as the other team members laughed, one of them clamping a yellow Post-It note over Ed's mouth. He shook it off with a grin. Ed Mulligan is a talented electronics engineer and a respected member of the team but known for his incessant wisecracking.

"The thing is," continued Jack, "all these articles start out saying more or less the same thing: 'Wouldn't it be nice if we could predict the future?' And then they go on as if it's just a rock solid 'given' that nobody can do that."

"Not unless you're an Old Testament prophet," said Ed, apparently using the Biblical reference in a clumsy attempt to redeem himself, so to speak.

"Maybe so, but our clients are reading this stuff day in and day out, so you know they're interested in it. And my question to you folks is, 'What if we *really could* predict the future?'"

Silence.

"This is where I came in," I said, rising as if to leave.

"Now you stop acting like Ed, Art!" said Anita with a smile.

"That's easy enough, but I'm not so sure about predicting the future. Are you serious, Jack? Okay, dumb question."

And it was. Jack can joke with the best of the Edwards of the world, but when it comes to business, he is a ser-i-ous man.

This was Anita's meeting, but Jack likes to drop in on the teams from time to time, hear what they have to say, ask a few questions, see if he can help. Not only is it great for morale, but he often comes up with advice and subtle redirection that leaves the teams more focused and charged up than if they were operating more independently, yet without undermining the team leaders. It's a wonderful talent.

"I've got another meeting, so just let me leave you with that for a week or so, and Anita maybe you can get back to me with whatever thoughts you all come up with."

With that, Jack put down his now half empty (or was it half full?) mug and was out the door.

"I think there's a big gauntlet on the floor in here somewhere," said Dr Judy Carter, a bio-tech expert.

"You're right," answered Anita, "and it probably has a new product idea clutched in it, but I sure don't know what it is yet."

"We'd better pick it up so we don't trip over it on the way out," said Ed with an uncharacteristically serious expression.

TWO: APP-GAP, INC.

You've never heard of App-Gap, Inc., because we fly under the radar. We're small, but we bill big, working for companies like Microsoft, Sony, Verizon, GE, car companies, big pharma and bio-techs, and so on. We inventory their product lines and look for better ways to tie them together or expand them. That's a gap analysis. Then we fill the gaps. Hence, App-Gap. Some of our work is mundane, but some is beyond state of the art. We're very good.

I'm Art Walters, the finance director and the closest thing to a Public Relations guy in a company that doesn't want any publicity. "Private Relations" doesn't say it either and is too much like "Internal Affairs," which always makes me think about checking the broom closets for people having more fun than they're supposed to during breaks. I attend most of the meetings Jack goes to, and I take good notes so we can document our decision making processes and keep track of intellectual property rights. That makes me sort of the company historian too. So if you are reading this then either you are an authorized App-Gapper or something has gone wrong.

You'd expect us to be in Silicon Valley, or maybe on Route 128 in

Massachusetts, but no, it's Greensboro, North Carolina, where the favorite pastimes are barbecue and college basketball. We rent space in a former textile mill that's home to a few startup companies and a couple of beauty salons. Even here we keep a low profile, displaying only a small "App-Gap, Inc." plaque beside our main entrance and encouraging our people to drive to work in cars at least five years old.

Our mailing address is a PO box. The guy who picks up the mail is a high school kid who works part time maintaining our computers and doesn't know much about what we really do. We are probably the only high tech company in the world that doesn't have a website.

THREE

Later that day, Anita appeared at my office wearing a conspiratorial expression.

"Can I come in?" she asked, furtively looking over her shoulder.

"Of course. What's up?"

She shut the glass-windowed door behind her, closing the little venetian blinds that, when open, guard against the appearance of sexual harassment, not there was likely ever to be any in this company. Certainly not in my office.

"I think Ed may already have the answer," she said, not sitting down.

"The answer to what?"

"You know. The thing Jack was talking about this morning."

"Oh." Then I remembered. "Oh! Okay. But why are you telling me? It's Jack's question."

"Right now I'm a little afraid to tell Jack. First of all, he gave us a week and it's only been four hours, so I don't want him to think we're not serious or that we're going off half crocked."

"Half cocked," I corrected.

"Whatever. Second, I don't want him to think we're crazy."

"Why would he think that?"

"Because, frankly, I'm not sure we're not."

"So you want to tell me first, is that it? Apparently, it's okay if I think you're crazy."

"Something like that." She sat down, smiling a little.

"And then if I don't think you're crazy, you'll want me to be there when you tell Jack because it's okay if he thinks *I'm* crazy."

"You're quick."

I am used to being kind of an ombudsman. Not that there is much conflict to resolve around here or that Jack is unapproachable, but people respect him a lot, so they want to be careful and very professional when presenting ideas or progress reports. For some reason, uptight people feel a little less uptight around me and will often use me as a sounding board, even though they know I'm close to Jack. I don't tell Jack everything, and he knows that, but never once has he said to me, "Are you sure there isn't something you're not telling me?"

"Okay, shoot," I said.

"Well, maybe we don't have 'The Answer' yet, but we do have a theory."

"'We?'"

"Well, mainly Ed, of all people."

"He can be serious when he needs to be," I said. "And he sure is smart."

"I agree, but at first I thought he was kidding when he told us how he thinks it might actually be possible to see into the future."

"Don't tell me he wants to build a time machine," I said.

"No, I think we can rule that out. Most scientists agree time travel is impossible."

I was kidding about the time machine. Anita wasn't.

"So what's Ed's idea?"

"Basically, he thinks that by using whatever we use to see into the past, our memory I guess, we can use the same thing to see into the future."

"And you think there's something to this?"

"Yes," she said evenly.

"Okay, you're right—I think you're crazy."

"No, you don't."

"No," I said, searching her face, which still looked troubled, "... I don't."

I got up and stared out the window for a moment and then turned back to Anita who was looking at me expectantly. "I can see why you're not ready to talk to Jack."

She seemed to relax a little at that, so I continued. "What's Ed doing now?"

"He said the idea sort of popped into his head just before the meeting broke up and he hasn't had time to think it through. He's spending the rest of the day outlining his thoughts for when we meet again in the morning."

"And you want me to be there."

"Could you?"

"Count on it."

FOUR

I was worried about the air of secrecy Anita was bringing to this thing. We work with an open team concept. A team is assigned to each project, its makeup of talents and skills based on the particular needs of the project. A person can be on as many as three or four teams at the same time, depending on the required skills, so it's important for the team leaders to get along with each other and coordinate their work schedules.

Bonuses are based more on how the whole company performs than on how an individual project fares. There is good-natured competition among the teams for innovation, quality of work, beating deadlines, coming in under budget, and so forth, but it's well understood that it's to nobody's advantage to keep secrets from each other about what the teams are doing. The collegial atmosphere makes it hard to keep secrets anyway and often leads to synergistic results, and that benefits everybody. Still, it would be imprudent to run up and down the halls broadcasting every new idea that occurs to you. Better to think it through, which is what Ed was doing.

FIVE

The next day was Supercasual Friday. We dress casual every day, but people in the businesses around us were more casual than usual. Flip-flops, cargo shorts and logo tee shirts. No Dilbert bathrobes, but still too casual even for us. I arrived at 8:30, checked my e-mail for important dispatches from the front, or from Jack. Finding nothing requiring my immediate attention, I joined Anita's team meeting, late again. Somebody had brought doughnuts to go with the coffee. I grabbed one and took a seat.

Besides Anita, Ed, and Judy the bio-tech specialist, there was Juan Chavez, a design engineer who fashions the cabinets and cases to house the circuitry of many of our apps. Their "clothing," as we call it. And Mike Morton, software programmer *par excellence*. Ed was handing out copies of what looked like a short presentation. Nobody sat in the captain's chair, out of respect for Jack. Which means he was there in spirit.

"This is still a little rough," Ed said with a smile. "I'd appreciate it if you'd follow along and not jump to the last page like Jack always does."

I looked to see if maybe Jack had quietly dropped in, but he hadn't.

"Okay, let me start with an analogy," Ed began, "which is what got me thinking about this in the first place. Imagine you're watching a

127

parade. It's been going on for a while, so lots of floats and marching bands have already gone by. Think of those as 'the past.' It has happened, and you remember it. What you see on the street right now is 'the present.' Say it's the back end of a float that's going away, another float in front of you and bunch of Shriners in little funny cars approaching. "The 'future' is what you can't see yet, beyond the funny cars. Okay so far?"

Everybody nodded.

"Okay. Now in this situation it is possible to predict the future at least a little bit. We use our senses to gather information and make deductions, sometimes augmented with assumptions based on logic or experience, and we come up with 'predictions.' For example, if you can hear drums in the distance from the direction of the parade's origin, you can 'predict' that another marching band is coming."

"I guess if it's the Thanksgiving Day parade you can predict that Santa Claus will be at the end of it too," said Anita.

"Yes, and that's a good example of using an experience, remembering what happened at last year's parade, or just knowing it's a tradition, and applying a logical assumption. However, it's not quite the same thing as predicting something you haven't really seen yet."

"But it's still valid, isn't it?"

"Yes it is. And we do the same thing in life, don't we? You see a plane descending toward the runway and you predict it will land."

Judy spoke up. "Yes, but if there's a flock of geese on the runway that you didn't see, that plane may have to go around again and may not land for a while."

"That's right," said Ed. "And so much for your 'prediction' too. But now think about this. No matter what you 'predicted,' whatever is, *is*, whether you predicted it or not."

"In other words, in the sense that it's going to happen anyway, it already exists somehow?" asked Judy.

"Exactly."

"So you're saying that the future already exists?" piped up Mike.

"I'm suggesting it, yes."

Ed lost his previous job after circulating a satirical memo about some of his company's procedures, which his boss took personally. Jack gave him a second chance at App-Gap, and because I knew how grateful Ed was, I knew he would never do anything to jeopardize his position here, and therefore I knew this theory he was explaining was not just some flight of fancy. Anita knew it too, as I suspect did everybody else.

"I don't think I get it yet," said Juan.

Juan and Mike are both reserved, not prone to jumping into a discussion without some reflection, but I could sense Mike's excitement. Mike was in a Methodist seminary until he felt the programmer's call of ones and zeroes, and apparently he sees no conflict between science and the Bible.

"Well then let me take the parade analogy a step further," said Ed. "You can turn to page two, but now that I'm into this I'm not sure how helpful the outline is going to be."

"But at least we'll all be on the same page," I said. Lame, but I couldn't resist.

"Wait—I thought I'm supposed to be the one making the wisecracks," said Ed.

"And we got tired of waiting for one," I said.

"Well, thanks, I guess. Now, moving right along, how about this? Suppose you are watching the parade from the MetLife blimp."

"This is getting weird," said Juan, looking around at everybody.

"No, no, it's fascinating," countered Mike. "Keep going."

"You are looking down from the blimp, which means you can see the whole parade at once. You can zoom in on any part of it. For somebody down on the street, whatever point you zoom in on is either the past, the present, or the future, depending on where that person is along the parade route. But in the blimp, since you see it all at once, there is no past or future. It's all the present. It all exists at the same time.

"Past, present, and future are expressions of time. Time is linear. So for the person on the street the parade is like a timeline," Ed continued, but then paused. "Quick, somebody say, 'From the blimp you can drop a rock on the tuba player and change the future!'"

The old Ed was back.

"Yeah, but that wouldn't help your analogy very much," said Mike.

"Right, so let's get to the point of all this. Which is what I already said: Maybe the future already exists. It's already there, 'happening,' or 'already happened,' I'm not sure which."

"So then it follows that …?" offered Mike.

"It follows that if you can remember the past, maybe there is a way to 'remember' the future," finished Ed.

Mike was sitting on the edge of his chair. He looked around the room at the other team members, clearly composing himself before saying something.

"You all know my church background," he began, "so I know you'll give me a pass on this if you think it sounds crazy. In fact, there is some theology, well a lot actually, to support the idea that the future and the past both exist, right now—that what's predicted to happen has, in some dimension or other, already happened."

Nobody said anything, so Mike continued.

"Let's say we believe God created everything, including time, and He is in control of the universe He created. If so, then we can picture Him 'up there' in his Heavenly blimp looking at His whole creation from beginning to end simultaneously."

People were shifting uncomfortably, but still nobody spoke.

"The picture resembles your parade, but with one key difference,"

Mike went on. "Which is, He is still creating. Which means He can change the past as well as change the future from one that might have come to pass to one that will. At the same time, He knows exactly what it will be, including that He will have changed it. A paradox, yes it seems so, but after all, He's God. It's one reason physicists think there are more dimensions than we know of. Some say as many as 10 or 12.

"So," Ed interjected, "God could drop a rock on the tuba player."

"God doesn't do that sort of thing, but yeah, He could."

"I hope nobody would pray for that anyway," said Juan.

"Okay then," said Ed, taking charge again, "we have here either an analogy—the parade—and a reality—God's perspective—or two analogies, but either way it helps explain the idea I'm proposing, so thanks, Mike."

"I sure hope we don't make God mad. I've got enough problems!" said Juan.

There were a few chuckles at that, but nobody thought Juan was really joking.

Anita jumped back in.

"I see your logic and not saying I agree or anything, but how do you propose we 'remember' the future?"

"This is where it gets fun," said Ed. "Do you remember that interface we developed for those VidTron virtual reality games last year?"

Everybody nodded.

"One of the main selling points was how much faster the kids wearing our gear could get to higher levels in the game versus the kids with last generation gear. How did we do that?"

"Brain waves and bio-feedback," said Judy.

"That's right," Ed continued. "The equipment strapped on your head is a modified electroencephalograph that reads brain waves

131

generated during play, isolates the ones involved with cognition, coordination and muscle memory, and feeds those back to the brain so they play 'louder' and loop onto themselves, causing quicker responses and more accurate moves with each iteration of an episode in the game.

"I'm suggesting we can use that same technology to recognize and isolate brain waves generated when you're remembering something."

"Yes," said Judy slowly, "I'm pretty sure we could do that."

"Good. Now here's the theoretical part. As we record those brain waves, we try to determine the mathematical expression of the memory process, or seeing into the past. Then if we re-write the algorithms to reverse the process and put those altered brain signals back into the mind, we might be able to see into the future, because it's a future that's already happened."

"So, you're talking about 'remembering forward,'" said Mike.

"Yes."

"Comments, anybody?" said Anita, looking around the room.

"Wow," said Juan.

"No, I really don't see any reason we can't do the math and reintroduce the results to the brain," said Judy.

"Wouldn't there be some risk of brain damage?" asked Mike.

"I'd want to set up some tests, of course," said Judy, "but I don't think we're talking about 'rewiring' the brain or anything like that, just feeding it some temporary information or stimuli. Really no different from reading a book or watching a movie, or any other experience, except it's directly applied instead of going through the senses." She paused thoughtfully. "There might be some 'learning' that takes place, just as with any experience, and of course the experience of 'remembering the future' itself will be added to the memory, but … I don't know … I guess we'll just have to see."

"Art?" said Anita. I knew what she meant.

"It doesn't sound like getting to the experimental stage would cost a lot of money, since we already have the basic technology and equipment anyway," I answered. "If you can sell Jack on this, I'll tell him we can afford it."

"Well then," Anita said, turning back to the team, "Ed, why don't you and Judy work up a development plan and a budget? Let's get together again on Wednesday morning to look at it, and meanwhile I'll schedule a meeting with Jack for Thursday."

"A week since the gauntlet hit the floor," said Ed.

"That's right. Can we do it?"

"I think so," said Ed, looking at Judy who nodded in agreement.

"Wow," said Juan.

SIX

The rest of the day was routine for me, and the weekend was pretty quiet. My wife and daughter and I took in a bluegrass concert at one of the local vineyards on Saturday and then went to church on Sunday, followed by lunch at a pancake house with some friends.

I was there on Thursday when Anita's team pitched their project to Jack. He liked it a lot. He even said, "Wow," which I'm sure made Juan's day.

The team was off and running. A special room was set aside for their exclusive use, which was not unusual for a new project. However, because of the unprecedented air of secrecy surrounding the project, people started referring to the room as "Area 61," a nod to the Air Force's famous "Area 51" in Nevada, where the dead UFO aliens are supposedly kept, but reflecting the assumption that App-Gap, after all, would only deal in a much more modern and sophisticated variety of science fiction. Hence the upgrade from "51" to "61."

SEVEN: AREA 61

Fast forward six weeks. Invited by Anita, I entered Area 61 for the first time. With blackout curtains covering the windows it took me a minute for my eyes to adjust. Ed stood next to something resembling a crude airport security screening machine, large and menacing, with a swivel chair under it and a red bicycle helmet dangling above that. Anita stood beside him. Mike, Judy and Juan sat before computers, looking at me with sly grins. There was a low but pervasive humming sound coming from somewhere.

"It's a mess, I know," said Anita, "but it's only temporary. We haven't let Juan loose on designing this equipment for market yet."

"What am I looking at?" I said.

"That's the 'hot seat,'" she said. "It's where you'll sit if you agree to be the first non-team member to test what we've got."

I felt like saying, "Wow" but refrained. "I suppose I should be honored, but let me ask you: Are you saying all of you have tested this thing?"

They all nodded.

"And you're all happy with it?"

More nods, this time with grunts of affirmation.

"Art, it's safe, if that's what you're getting at. At least as far as we can tell."

"And believe me, we've taken every precaution and run every test we could think of," added Judy. "We're all still here, we're all still sane, and nobody's memory has been wiped, right, Ed?"

"Uh, say what?" said Ed.

I ignored Ed's obviously rehearsed response, knowing these people are smart and careful, not reckless. I knew I could trust them, but still …

"Would *monsieur* care to take his seat upon the throne?" asked Ed with a grand gesture toward the chair.

I sat. Ed put the bicycle helmet on my head.

When I'm telling this story now, usually at this point I'll say, "And I don't remember anything else after that. Hey, where am I?" There will always be a moment of confused silence, and then people will either laugh or groan. I tell them it was Ed's idea, which is true, and that he planted it in my brain sort of like a post-hypnotic suggestion. Which might be true. I don't know.

Anyway, then Ed said, "We'll start with some easy exercises first, just to get you used to how this works."

"Okay."

"I want you to remember walking through the door here a few minutes ago. Can you go back and try to picture that in your mind? What you saw, what you heard, anything else you remember."

"You mean right at that instant?"

"Yes, that plus the first few seconds after you came in, you know, that short period of time."

"Okay, I'm now remembering that."

"Good."

Ed did something with what looked like a TV remote. The humming noise got louder for a moment and then subsided.

I noticed a lot of new activity on nearby computer screens. Judy and Anita, seated now, were busy typing on their keyboards. Then Anita nodded to Ed.

"All right, we've taken the data we recorded while you were remembering and we've massaged it, and now I'm going to send the new data into your brain. It will only take a split second. You won't feel anything, but you might think you are seeing something. If you do, please do not tell us what you see. Okay?"

"Okay."

Ed fingered the remote again, and I saw a weird double scene with two of everybody and then the kid who delivers the mail came in, handed Anita a large manila envelope, and left, which hadn't happened when I was coming in. Then things went back to normal. I looked around and didn't see a large manila envelope anywhere. Maybe Anita had put it in a drawer.

"Are you okay, Art?" asked Ed.

"Yeah, I think so, but …"

"No, don't say anything. Unless you don't feel well or something."

"I feel fine."

"Good. So, Mike, how long ago now did Art come into the room?"

"About three minutes ago," answered Mike.

"Okay, then," said Ed, looking at his watch, "let's just sit tight here for a while."

I looked at my watch too, there being nothing else to do just then.

After two and a half minutes, here came the kid "again" with his envelope. I'm finding it hard to write about this without making it sound like a comedy skit. You can't make this stuff up.

Ed and Anita both must have seen something in my expression because they both said, "What?"

"Can I talk now?"

"Yes!" they practically shouted, "Talk!"

"I already saw what just happened. I mean I saw it two and a half minutes ago, only it seemed like I had seen it before, even then."

"Like a memory?" asked Anita, now holding the envelope.

"That's a leading question, but yeah, like that. And then, just now, it was like a *déjà vu* of *déjà vu*," I said.

"Like '*déjà vu* all over again,' as the saying goes," quipped Ed.

"And I just have to believe that's the first time you've said that in all of the past six weeks," I replied.

Juan didn't say, "Wow."

"If you're up for it, I want us to run two more exercises. These will give us longer timelines, and you can come back later and tell us what you experienced."

Ed asked me to remember having breakfast that day. I did, and we went through the same steps, me in the hot seat with the helmet, but I wasn't sure I was getting anything that time. My mind kept wandering to a meeting downtown I was scheduled to have that afternoon for which I hadn't yet fully prepared. I could expect some confusion and disappointment on the part of the other people at the meeting if I didn't have my ducks in a row, but sometimes I'm a little paranoid that way.

After that, Ed asked me to pick an event of my own choosing to remember, but it had to be something within the past week. He handed me a pad and pen to jot it down but not show it to anyone. The event and about how long ago it had been. I recalled coming out of Home Depot the previous Saturday morning, four days before, and finding a sizeable ding in the right front door of my car. Whoever did it didn't leave a note, and I was moderately steamed even though the car has plenty of other battle scars. I wrote all that down, keeping it to myself, and we went through the process again, during which I recalled that my pastor had talked about the importance of forgiveness in his sermon on Sunday.

After that chastening thought it was time to leave. I took off the helmet, "thank you's" were exchanged all around, and *monsieur* guinea pig took his leave of Area 61 and went back to my office.

EIGHT

You've probably guessed what happened next. My afternoon meeting was a disaster, by my standards anyway. I never did find enough time to get ready for it. I thought I could "wing it," but I had to field some questions I didn't have the answers to, and it just created confusion. Finally, I had to ask everybody if we could schedule a re-do the following week. They were disappointed, but they agreed.

And it came to pass on Sunday that my pastor delivered a strangely familiar sermon on forgiveness, one I am not likely to forget soon, since I've "heard" it twice.

Now that I had been co-opted into Anita's camp by my experience in Area 61, she felt it was time to go to Jack for major development funds to commercialize the phenomenon. Naturally, he wanted to try out the booth himself. He did so on Tuesday, took home a summary of the team's findings from the previous month and a half of testing, waited a week to see if whatever he "remembered" of the future came true, and then summoned Anita and me.

"So how much will this cost?" Jack asked.

Anita told him. I gulped silently.

"Art, can we afford that?"

"Well, uh …"

"Okay then, Anita. That's your budget."

I made a note.

Things moved quickly after that. The lawyers had questions, so I sent them to Anita and Ed. Mike was the first to call it the Prophecy Booth. It was just a passing reference during some banter with Ed. We all laughed, but the name stuck. Juan finished the design work and produced handmade versions along with specs for the molds and dies needed for production later.

The team spruced up Area 61, and Jack began inviting selected clients to test the new device on a confidential basis. And no matter how important they were or how big their egos, Jack insisted they all arrive and leave in taxis, not rock star limousines.

I visited Area 61 often enough over the next few months to become annoying since I didn't have much to contribute, but I was tolerated. I did notice that when clients came in to test the Booth, most of the time they left smiling. Anita seemed happy too, so apparently development was progressing well and there were no surprises, at least not bad ones.

I'm not sure how all the clients were using the Booth when they tested it, and I don't claim to understand all this well enough to explain it myself, but according to Ed there is theoretically no limit to what you can remember of the future once you learn a few tricks. Yes, it's possible to "remember" who will win the Kentucky Derby or the World Series so you can bet on it and make some money, but we presume our clients have more lofty goals. They're interested in whether the economy will go up or down, what new laws will be passed, maybe what the weather is going to do, what their competitors are going to come out with, and that sort of thing. Important stuff. Some were apparently benefitting quite well already, if you went by their stock prices, so I know they had learned to extend the scope of their memories far beyond what they had for breakfast last Thursday.

The team focused on honing the device's accuracy and ease of use, but I can tell you Jack was well aware of the larger implications of this invention. I sat in long discussions with the lawyers not only about intellectual property rights, but also the serious ethical considerations involved, not to mention those of national security, especially if the government, ours or anybody's, or criminals, got wind of it and decided the Prophecy Booth would somehow make a great weapon. At this point, I'm not going to divulge what strategies they came up with to protect us as long as possible from chaos. We'll have to wait some time before there is enough history with the Booth to turn this story into a novel. However, I do know Jack had used the Booth himself to look ahead with these questions in mind, and he seemed satisfied we were safe to proceed, at least for a good while longer.

I wasn't so sure.

NINE

On a Friday afternoon, Jack asked the whole company to gather in Area 61. The air had been electric for several days. Everybody knew something was up, and probably something good, but since Friday is the traditional day for bad news in corporate America, Supercasual Fridays notwithstanding, there was still a certain level of anxiety as we all trooped in. Everyone found seats, including Jack who had refrained from bringing his antique captain's chair from the conference room and sat on a rickety folding chair like the rest of us. The blackout curtains were gone, and the room was bright, the Booth occupying center stage, strikingly illuminated by the sunlight pouring in. When everybody was settled, Jack stood up.

"Who called this meeting, anyway?" he began.

Nobody laughed.

"Okay, I'll try again," he said. "As you may know, I've anticipated a meeting like this for quite some time."

That brought some groans and snickers as people glanced from Jack to the Booth. Jack looked slightly bewildered in the instant it took him to realize what he'd said.

"Oh. No, what I meant was it's always been my dream for this company to be not just a success, but a roaring big hairy audacious success, and for all of us to benefit from the hard work we've put into it. So I've been looking forward to someday making an announcement like the one I'm about to make. It's good news. You will like it."

"Well, what is it?" shouted Ed, unable to contain himself any longer.

"This magical device you see before you, this thing we call the Prophecy Booth, is like a lottery ticket. And we've won the lottery."

By now, everyone in the company had been clued in to what was going on in Area 61. That was just part of our culture, and indeed several people not on the original team had offered input and suggestions that improved the Booth's performance. Everybody felt some ownership in the project, so Jack didn't have to explain that again. But he did have to get them off the edges of their flimsy folding chairs before they all fell on the floor.

"We've just signed long term contracts with four of our biggest clients for rights to use the Booth. We're expecting three more to sign up within a few weeks. These contracts call for very large up-front payments for exclusive rights on an industry by industry basis, where we won't sign clients who compete with each other. Besides the large retainers there are separate charges for each time a client uses the Booth."

Mouths were hanging open, but so far none of the chairs had collapsed.

"That means we're going to need seven Booths in addition to this one so each client can have one dedicated to his own use. That will keep you pretty busy for a while, Juan."

"Wow," said Juan, predictably.

"Client CEOs are the only people authorized to use the Booths, and they all have to come here to do it. We've established severe financial penalties for breaches of confidentiality. We can't let this technology get out of the building, and we need to keep it as quiet as possible, although I know it's only a matter of time before there will be leaks. But those leaks are not going to come from us, right?"

"Right!" the room shouted back.

"Now here's what you've been waiting to hear," Jack continued. "There will be surprisingly large bonuses for everyone, beginning as soon as the big money starts coming in. We won't wait until the end of the year. And just as long as the prosperity continues, and I have every reason to believe it will ..." At this, he winked. "... so will the bonuses."

The applause was deafening even though there were only twenty-five people, but it was a fairly small room.

"Naturally, thanks go to Anita and her team. Edward, Mike, Judy, Juan, please stand."

Somewhat sheepishly but with cat-who-ate-the-canary grins, they stood to more applause, then sat.

"And the rest of you as well. Your hard work on our other projects kept the company going long enough to get us to this point. Thank you! And by the way, work on the other projects will continue, and we'll be looking for more new business just as we always have. We may have won the lottery, after a fashion, but I'm having way too much fun to quit!"

After the meeting everyone milled around for a while, congratulating each other, some making furtive cell phone calls, and others lovingly touching the Booth as if it were a giant talisman.

TEN

The next several weeks were a blur of activity as Juan prepared more Booths and the team wrote protocol for how they would be used by the clients. As Booths became ready, client CEOs made appointments, arrived and left in a sort of parade. I imagined God looking down on all of this, knowing the beginning and the end, but not letting us in on it except that He had given Ed the inspiration for the Booths in the first place. The App-Gap bank account ballooned.

Someone suggested we should buy stock in our client companies, but Jack insisted that would be considered insider trading. There was no need to get greedy.

ELEVEN

One morning on a day when very nice articles about two of our clients appeared in *The Wall Street Journal*, I heard a soft, almost tentative, knock on my office door. It was Anita, looking even more distressed than when she had first come to tell me about the idea that had set all this in motion. She came in and closed the door, and the venetian blinds, and sat.

142

"You don't look so good," I said. "What's wrong?"

"I don't know who else to tell," she murmured. "I was going over the math again last night for the umpteenth time, because all this is still so unbelievable."

"Well, that's your job, isn't it?"

"Of course, and I don't mean to obsess about it, but here's the thing. I found a mistake, and I don't know what to do about it."

"What do you mean you found a mistake?"

"I mean I've run the numbers a thousand times since this started, and they always made sense, until last night when I found a mistake. I don't know if it was a typo in the original equations or what, but I'm telling you the math is wrong. This shouldn't be working." Anita sat down.

"But it *is* working. Right?" I said.

She nodded. "But there's more ..."

"Like what?"

"People who have used the Booth a lot are starting to see into the future without it. If that keeps up, they aren't going to need us anymore!"

That was about a week ago. Anita still hasn't decided what to do. Some of our people have ordered Ferraris and Lamborghinis and are shopping for beachfront property, in the Caymans. Even the kid who picks up the mail has made a down payment on a new SUV.

Nobody knows yet that a rock has been dropped on the tuba player.

As I said, I don't tell Jack everything. At least not right away. Besides, shouldn't he have seen this coming?

143

Paleontology
A poem of science and old fashioned romance

Hidden treasures allured me when I was a pup;
while the other kids played with their toys,
buried mine in my sandbox and then dug them up.
I wasn't like most other boys.

Then dinosaurs surfaced and changed me for good,
gave me something to dig that was real.
Don't make me play baseball; I'm not in the mood,
for it's fossils not bases I'll steal.

"In paleontology he's a child prodigy,"
teachers would whisper in awe,
for even though petrified I could identify
fragments of femur or jaw.

But I've lived in a graveyard for all of my life
with degrees and awards on my shelf
while the world passed me by and my work was my wife.
Now I'm facing extinction myself.

My friends are all married, but I'm all alone,
and my life is as dry as a bone.
Too long I have tarried; it's time to atone:
need to dig up a wife of my own.

I'll find me a mate if I'm cautious yet bold;
it's time some tame oats I was sowing.
Although I'm quite old, my passion's not cold,
and we'll start a family growing.

I've been sleeping for eons and failing to see
what I've missed is much more than a mile.
Waking up to find out Rip van Winkle is me,
and my phone has a rotary dial.

No Internet, e-mail or YouTube for me,
and fat screen describes my TV.
No iPad, no laptop, no desktop PC,
and Facebook? Well, Twitter dee dee.

While the women are many whom I'd like to meet,
I've no iPhone or Berry that's Black,
so most of them think that I'm too obsolete,
and they don't bother calling me back.

But still, say I, I'm a digital guy –
See my fingers and sharp graphite pencil?
I'll walk through the phone book and also apply
my opposable thumbs quite prehensile.

What I seek is quite rare and she cannot compare
to a woman who's just ordinary.
Not a gold digger here or a sourpuss there
or a girl who's still too young to marry.

Long courtship's a luxury I can't indulge.
At my age I've no time to waste.
But to geezers like me women hate to divulge
their vital statistics in haste.

I want a good woman who's close to my age,
but a facelift can mask what I'm getting.

So which way to go and what is my gauge?
What tools can I use in the vetting?

I can't tell by her teeth what lies underneath,
for horses and women aren't equal.
I need something foolproof the truth to unsheathe:
Spring chicken or biddy deceitful?

Ah, there is one antiquely professional skill
the decades have proven infallible –
A special technique that should fill the bill –
it's simple, unique and available.

It's a poor last resort, but I'll get a report
and at last put an end to my waiting.
An error to thwart and avoid divorce court –
I'll just say it: I'm carbon dating.

When Superheroes Learn to Fly, Part 2

(Memorialized in clerihew)

SuperGirl
Had a feminist whirl.
"If Clark can fly,
Then so must I."

Spider Man
Was not in great demand
Until he honed his webbed ministrations,
Sensing tacky foes to put in sticky situations.

Wonder Woman
Is a female airman.
Her invisible jet
Flies her anywhere she needs to get.

The Incredible Hulk
Is never one to merely sulk.
He wears his feelings on his shredded sleeve,
Can't fly but jumps so high you won't believe.

Iron Man
Can't get a tan.
He's head to toe in metal,
A repulsor-propelled flying kettle.

Batman
Is a rich man.
He bought the means by which to fly,
A hang-gliding cape not sold to you and I.

The Silver Surfer,
What's he here fer?
On his super surfboard faster than light,
He's useless since he's always out of sight.

The Nite Owls
Fighting crime most foul:
Not happy as one vigilante,
As two they steeply up the ante.

The Flying Nun
Inhabits so much fun.
Her starched cornette lifts like a kite;
When she's in flight it's quite a sight.

Fly Man, Tommy Troy,
Summoned Turan while a boy
With a fly-shaped emblem stolen from his boss
And learned that the evil-fighting Fly People once ruled the earth and
now that they don't anymore it's our loss.

G-Girl
Makes me want to hurl.
Her superpowers are abused
When by her boyfriend she's refused.

Storm
Is surprisingly close to the norm.
She stirs up wind to give her wings
Like politicians when they do their things.

The Flying Friar
Narrowly escaped the pyre.
'Twas witchcraft 'til they said it ain't;
Giuseppe's now a patron saint[1].

Santa Claus
We love because
He brings us stuff,
But we can never get enough.

Hercule Poirot
Just minces to and fro.
Fly?
Why?

Poetry Exercise:
Don't see your favorite superhero here? Maybe it's because he or she can't fly or is instead a supervillain. Still, feel free to add whomsoever you wish and make up your own clerihew. It's an easy, fun form of poetry with few rules, invented by humorist Edmund Clerihew Bentley when he was a schoolboy in London around 1891. Go ahead, write one, or several. Impress your friends with your new-found literary prowess.

[1]Joseph of Cupertino (Italy) 1603-1663. Known for levitating and ecstatic visions. Now Patron Saint of air travelers, aviators, astronauts, the mentally handicapped, and poor students. Go figure.

Day of the Philosophy Thing
Nietzsche, eat'cher heart out!

Differential Overview of Bounds within the Religion of the Analytic, or Categorically Metaphysical – A Philosophical Treatise

(Originally published in *Worm Runner's Digest*, 1974, Vol. 16, No. 2, *Journal of Biological Psychology*, University of Michigan [Ann Arbor])

"Behold! Forth-trembling, it is like unto the tribulation of the Word withal. Stand in silence when one is not allowed? Ridiculous!"

– Aristaphiabaldistaphenes

This philosophical treatise will of course seem to some as if it is not all that which one might expect from the initiation of such a work under the conditions as yet unspecified by the conscience. Nevertheless, it is hoped that the work will not be unduly received or critically signified. The dichotomy which exists after the fact of other considerations should not impair categorical apprehensions suggested by possible further revisions of present attitudes. Whenever one sets out to make the ensuing plausible juxtapositions, this problem and its evident variations are always in view.

Necessarily, there exists a multitude of dissenters to this opinion. But if it were to be presented out of the context of our presently considered matrix of understanding, the situation might well be otherwise unless our perceptions permitted this to no avail, considering the results.

Finally, if we must epitomize only for the sake of clarification, let us do so without fear of contradiction, lest our purpose be obscured.

Denial of Dualisms

1. The anticipatory goal in our present study is the allaying of the mono-didacticism basic to our nature, forming a mental triumvirate. Of these, five can readily be discerned and examined. There is, however, no immediate need for amplification unless the understanding wanes, in which case we would retract substantially, keeping always the firm footing on our position of ancillary uncooperativeness regarding the disagreement for which it stands. We are reminded of the evolution of subjective internalism as father of abverse progression, having similar implications.

2. If these dualisms are to be allowed to exist, with how, then, are they to be dealt? Surely there is not one among us who would refuse conjugation in time of need. But if we presuppose after the fact, the argument turns on a consideration of abverse progression in terms of ethical expanse or discriminantly. Therefore, it is possible to prove a justification after all. Let the others find it; it is none of our concern. It is only the esoteric communication when used alterably or not which enables the few who choose to refrain from it. Even Adam Smith disagreed. But I digress.

3. A note on syndactyl and cleaved imagery reveals that trampling on the grapes of desire with feet of clay will not cause the wine of sobriety to flow. We must not yield.

4. It is axiomatic that the existence of the transcendent precludes dissension in the peremptory unless challenged. But we should not be agitated by those who profess in the affirmative and then deny without sufficient grounds. A dualism does not exist on these grounds either, and we can deny it. We need not worry about history in this respect, of course, because, as we know, history is rapidly becoming a thing of the past.

Eventual Philosophical Necessity

5. In order to prescribe a basis for tangible justification in the matter of eventual necessity (as opposed to necessary eventuality), it eventually becomes necessary to do so with a minimum undertone of the meaning itself. Forgetting for a moment the inferred utility of deistic consideration so prevalent in our mores, we should familiarize outright. In the words of Locke, "Sooner or later we will wish we had."[1]

6. When one assumes license in these matters, there is, consequently, an immediate trend toward extra moral sensitivity on the parts of those injectivists who advocate the primary as their mode of ideal in the main. Their justification rests beside itself through time, which is, after a fashion, the first fledgling attempt at full realization. We almost hesitate, anticipating the vague duration, to drag out the age-old example of the man who, when he saw his brother unjustly beaten and strangled, rose up in defiance of the act so perpetrated and vile and was rewarded with immense spiritual uplift and anachronism, which was his favorite.

7. Take, for another example, music. No, actually that is not a very good example.

8. We recall Hume's viewpoint on eventual necessity as manifested in his writing, on the one hand. (Hume was also known for other peculiar habits.) It is impossible to destroy without altering the fastidiousness of an assumption so arranged and having such unproven but liable virtuosity. Not surprisingly, Kant's view of equality was the same.

9. We have achieved the first of our goals, and it now remains merely to effect translation along an inerrant plan to obliterate the aggregate in essence. There is a sense in which we attempt to run the full gamut of aspiration. Likewise, a paradox exists. Then let

it remain so, for we have that which passes for necessity in the guise of that which does not, excluding, of course, consideration of the significance of any arbitrary flexible margin.[2]

A. In Man

10. Man's position, relative undoubtedly, is probably best summed up: "He who stumbles and falls by the wayside shall forever remain under the squalor of the unwarranted, unto death or its alternative, should this in the first place happen to him."

B.In Nature

11. Here is the seat of the squalor. Wayside is the keyword in our understanding here. If we are able to adapt constructively, we must purposely place an obstacle in the path of our endeavors to strive incessantly and relentlessly to stop. We must test ourselves, with this sufficing as the universal "out." "Wayside" as synonymous with "outside" gives us these two words and no more. If we allow the two roots ("side") to cancel each other out, we will have left the two prefixes, the conjunction of which naturally follows. To back up this observation and its implications, we have the reassuring words of Saint Seymour: "That's exactly the way I would have explained it."[3]

The Dawn of Particular Understanding

12. Similarly, vast exemptions exist whose corollaries undermine all anthropological interstices in the tertiary scheme. In other words, seven seemingly unrelated particulars are shown conclusively to be at the apogee of the basic impunitive. Our argument thus rests on a similar perusal underlying the usual sanguinity associated with function in the traditional incarnate. Its true and lasting implications are only now beginning to be understood, however inarticulately

opposed to comprehension. Verily, it is Veblen, the veritable forefather of this school of thought, who, speaking from the old easy chair he loved so well, might have said, "Damn the canons (sic)."[4]

13.   True, other considerations must be added in spite of gathering hypocrisy in the flow of necessity. And unless it is pertinent, a forced commission of intricacies staggers the imagination even as it would if not. Thoroughly trebled, the allusion is almost perfect, even as the sun rises in the east. [5]

A. The Unique Commonplace in Experience

14.   But let us not be too hasty in our evaluation of extraneous pertinence regarding domestic and metamorphic solidification of our theory until it is clearly indicative. Experience, as phenomenon, is as we know it to be, of course. We are indeed becoming morally warm in our quest for the nebulous and stringent, however inclined. Should this fail, there is the obvious. But let us not entangle ourselves in detail, since brevity is of the essence if our aim is to be the facilitation of clarity. Our consoling salve originates in the *raison d'etre est amasser des femmes et le pillage* method practiced by the Huns who, because they unfortunately did not speak French, did not know what they were doing.

B. Inverse Sexuality: The Imperative Category

15.   The method of gauging metriculate rotundity varies with the inverse square of the ocular. However, sexually there are two. When severally understood, the metaphysical ramifications of repression run definitely counter. And, as must all epistemological ceremonies advocating mingled propensities, these must be kept in context with the whole. These are the principles by which we must live.

157

Conclusion

We are reminded of the parable of the young man who, when asked what he meant by a particularly subtle comment, replied, "Nothing," and was committed then to the flames.

Our goal has loomed and shaken off the fetters of disparity. Fortunately, the subject matter of our treatise allowed a measure of preliminary vacillation before conclusively passing from each to the next point. With this flexibility, an efficient machination transpired to a successful end, and therefore was allowed to grow at a substantial rate for a work so developed, considering the whole of the Western World. Furthermore, we agree, as did Glaucon.

While our program promulgated itself, there may be instances whereby gain can be made by simply remaining motionless relative to the empirical, but in a state of turgid animation regarding normative considerations – all things considered, perhaps a fitting subject for our next treatise.

ENDNOTES

[1] Spoken, unfortunately, in another context.

[2] 1n 1923 a struggling, young, free-lance philosopher named Haggis used the example of the elephant with a tumor to illustrate this point. Too bad the example was so disgusting that it never became very popular. Haggis starved to death in 1925.

[3] One of the famous "Tainted Saints," about whom very little has been written.

[4] It is a matter of grave moral concern whether Veblen should himself have footnoted this phrase when he used it in his little-known monograph, "The Leisure Class Revisited" (a study of the particularly sluggish sophomore class of 1901 at the University of Chicago), for its meaning is unclear. No one knows whether he meant to imply criticism of (a) cooperation between church and state, (b) a wasteful defense budget, or (c) sheets and towels.

[5] Based on empirical evidence. However, this statement appears to be valid only in the morning.

The Religion Student

"I quit!" said the e-mail.

It wasn't the first time Professor Miller had resigned, but it needed to be the last. Either he really meant it this time or I'd convince him to stop crying wolf once and for all. But I didn't know just how. Threatening to fire him didn't seem like the best move.

At least he hadn't "flamed" me by punching it all out in capital letters like students sometimes do when they're upset about something but are afraid to face me in person. I don't think I'm so unapproachable, notwithstanding the "Dean Doom" nickname given me by those I've disciplined. It's a play on Dominick Dooney, my real name. I'm supposed to hate it, but I think it's pretty clever. I know I'm tough, but I'm fair. We're building a good reputation here at Willoughby Community College, so I do have standards to uphold.

Like not letting problems fester too long. I picked up the phone, hoping to catch Miller still in his office.

"Looks like we need to talk, Pete." I said when he answered after five rings.

"Yeah, I guess you're right," he said in a lifeless voice. "No, I know you're right. Can I come over now?"

Peter Miller, Master of Divinity and Ph.D., has spent four years on the faculty. He's done a good job of building our social studies department, and in the process we've become good friends. World religions is his specialty, and he teaches a popular survey course on it. He's not a true academic, but he's well qualified in my opinion, being a retired minister from a mainline denomination, Presbyterian as I recall. He's a good department head and a good teacher, but the teaching part has its frustrations.

"Pearls before swine!" he shouted, bursting into my office.

"And good afternoon to you, too," I countered, smiling.

"Sorry, Dom. How is *your* day going?" He closed the door and sat down in the famously uncomfortable straight back chair across from my desk.

"Fine so far, thank you. I take it yours hasn't been the best?"

"Sheesh, but it never changes," he said. "I swear, I just don't know anymore …"

"Well, before you smite somebody, including me, even in an e-mail, let me guess: Student compliance not up to your expectations again?"

"Not even close, Dom. They just don't give a d-, I mean they just don't care. God forbid they should actually *study* once in a while!" His body slumped a little, about as much as is possible in that chair.

"Are you really going to quit?"

"No."

"Then will you quit threatening to quit? It makes it hard to plan." He laughed.

"I'm serious though, Pete."

"I know. And I'm sorry."

"You've been sorry before. It's not easy to say this but, friend or no friend, Peter Miller, one more threat and I'll have to accept it. Your resignation, I mean."

"All right, I understand. No more false alarms. Next time I say I'm going to quit it will be because I mean it. And I'll do it in person."

"Promise?"

"You have my word," he said, the seriousness back in his face. That was good enough for me.

"Okay, then. Now what set you off this time? Anything I can really help you with?"

He thought for a long moment before answering.

"You know, my biggest thrill as a teacher comes when one of my students 'gets it.' It's the main thing I live for in this job. Doesn't happen as often as I'd like, but when it does happen it makes up— well, almost makes up—for all the times the students don't care enough even to try.

"I mean, why are they here anyway?" he went on. "I thought it was to get prepared to make their way in the real world, like in a profession or at least a better job. We're supposed to be turning out people who will make a difference. Or helping them get ready to go to a university and get a degree."

"All of the above," I offered. "Willoughby looks good on a résumé or a college application, and I work hard to make sure we offer courses that match the needs of the business community."

"And yet I have the feeling half the men in my class are just there to meet women, and vice versa."

"Think of it as a lab in extracurricular life skills," I suggested. "No credit hours, but no additional tuition either."

"Ha! Well, I work hard too, Dom. I do."

There it was: the real problem. Now that I had taken off my Dean Doom hat, it was time to do a little stroking.

"Yes, you do work hard. You're a credit to Willoughby, a real asset. Your lectures are fun, but they're also deep, and I really don't believe your students are there just to be entertained. You know your 'Religions around the World' course is legendary, and we can't always accommodate everybody who signs up for it."

"I *am* proud of that," he said, sitting up a little straighter. "I use the best text book I can find, and the lectures are pretty good, if I do say so myself. Thirty years of preaching wasn't wasted. And even though

I make it clear that I'm a Christian, I want my students to think for themselves. They don't have to agree with me to get a good grade."

"Right, but you still haven't told me what happened."

"There's this one student. A young woman. She seems really interested in the subject. She listens in class, and I can see her taking notes. In class discussions it's obvious she's read the assigned chapters. And I keep thinking, 'She's getting it, she's *getting* it!'"

"And?"

"Today she asked for a conference after class, and I was happy to agree, so after everybody left we stayed in the classroom to talk.

"'Professor Miller,' she says, 'I've really enjoyed the class. I came to Willoughby to learn some things I need to know so I don't, like, make a fool of myself when I apply for jobs and stuff. And this class about all the different world religions has really made me think.'"

"Sounds like you've been getting through to her," I suggested.

"And then she says, 'It's made me see I need to decide which religion is best for me.'"

"Sounds even better," I said with cautious optimism. "Maybe she really *is* getting it."

"But then she says, 'You know, like, which one will look good on my résumé and everything.'"

"Uh-oh …"

"Yeah, and it gets worse," said Pete. "She says, 'Like, if I pick the wrong religion, what will people think?' And I say, 'Do you really think that's very important?' 'Well, duh …' she says.

"Then I say, 'Okay, but I'm still not sure how I can help you.'

"'You're very nice,' she says, 'and you're older and seem very wise, and you're an expert and everything, so I was hoping you could just give me some advice.'

"I say, 'I'll try, but you know I can't tell you what religion you should follow or what you should believe in.'

162

"'Oh, don't worry about that. I think I can decide for myself.'

"'That's a relief!'

"'You're a saint, Professor Miller! So, I've listened to your really good lectures and I've read the whole book and ... and well, it wasn't easy, you know, but I think I've finally got it narrowed down. I'm trying to decide whether to become, like, either a Christian or a Jew or a Muslim.'

"Then she looks me right in the eye, sincerity oozing from every pore, and she says, 'So, Professor Miller, my question is, what would Jesus do?'"

Sunrise Service

(Originally published in *Ancient Paths Literary Magazine*, April 2014)

In this photo, Pastor Will is reading his sermon to those of us in his congregation who had managed to get up early enough to attend the outdoor Sunrise Service. It was March and still very cold, so everyone had to bundle up. Except Pastor Will, who felt that wearing an overcoat over his fine black suit would somehow diminish his authority. For him, The Suit was like the clerical robes our denomination used to favor for ministers until they were abandoned in a nod to modernity and "relevance," whatever that means. At least he allowed the choir you see behind him to wear jackets.

We had been standing there on the church lawn a long time already, furtively stamping our feet to keep the circulation going. The big problem was that even though it was billed as the Sunrise Service, the sun was showing no sign of cooperating. In fact, it was beginning to snow. Knowing Pastor Will, I'll bet he was thinking, "If Moses could part the Red Sea, why can't I make the sun come up this morning of all mornings?"

I was just wishing he would let his people go.

Beginning

Resolved to try some verse,
her pen and paper poised
and heart's door open to rehearse.

Pent up muses favor this intention.

First a zephyr, then a breeze as thoughts flow freely to the page.
Rhyme and meter rise to greet her;
fear of failure won't defeat her.
Phrase on phrase with growing ease, adventure of a someday sage,

and virgin poet's triumph of invention.

Poem Paradise

I wonder where old poems go to die …
Or do they have a life that's not their own,
a different fate from things of flesh and bone,
not fade away nor vanish in the sky?
Is poem heaven like the one we know –
All imperfections edited divine,
all meter, rhyme and cadence in align,
so close to God in perfect form and flow?
Or maybe freedom reigns in such a place
with structure cast aside like shackles tossed
away along with criticism's cost
as if abandon won't in fact abase.
But truths once written never will be gone.
Not buried with their authors, they live on.

Promise

Originally published in *Fresh Magazine*, October 2012

A winter's promise
When sleeping trees remember
The springtime to come

Fields

It was one of those early summer evenings that feel lavender.
I must have read that somewhere because I don't know how lavender
feels.
If it does.
We were in Provence gazing at vast violet-gray fields of flowers that
she said were lavender.
Dilly, dilly.

There were perfume factories nearby, or, *s'il vous plaît, les parfumeries.*
Were there unseen fields of other flowers?
Roses, clover, jasmine,
dandelions? (No, that's wine – another part of France,
near Burgundy)

Anyway, in a perfumery gift shop she went nuts,
buying gifts for every woman she could think of
but surprisingly little for herself.

Later at the little restaurant near our little hotel,
needing to show off my little French, I ordered what I recognized on
the menu,
Les artichauts, which I don't like.
Is an artichoke a flower?
We've seen Castroville, California, "The Artichoke Center of the World."
Saw vast green-gray fields of bushes on an early summer evening that
felt artichoke.
Maybe there were some artichokeries nearby,
but we didn't buy anything

Nevermore

Nevermore will the sunshine pour over the rain,
nor for me will the flowers be open again.
And I'll see no more rainbows in skies up above,
nevermore taking joy in the arms of your love.

There's a place far away where lost lovers have gone,
when the ways of the world sing a bright siren song.
I can see them adrift on that far distant shore.
It's the land of lost lovers that's called Nevermore.

Nevermore will I hold you from sunset 'til dawn,
as we dance in the moonlight 'til all fears are gone.
Oh my passion will smolder but nevermore burn,
for I'll ne'er love another lest you should return.

There's a place far away where lost lovers have gone,
when the ways of the world sing a bright siren song.
I can see them adrift on that far distant shore.
It's the land of lost lovers that's called Nevermore.

Plethora

A plethora of words across a page,
whether written by a hack or by a sage,
can make a run-on sentence of Biblical proportions
it may require wit and punctuational contortions
to keep the flow of writing
consistently exciting
as it tells its own story adding parts to a whole
like an actor in a play performing every role,
and for literary minds it must ring true
if it aims to satisfy when the words accrue.

Help from the Government

Is it possible?

The National Bureau of Mellow Standards

By now you've probably noticed that the metric system hasn't caught on in America. In fact, we will probably all become left-handed sooner than we will bother to learn it.

There are several reasons for this. First, there is the "Buy American" feeling that makes us want to resist foreign imports like this. Also, we can't drive it, ride it, listen to it, watch it, Tweet it, or blast aliens with it, and it's just plain inconvenient to learn. Furthermore, it's too precise, which goes against the independent nature of most Americans. We don't like being told exactly how to do things, especially by the government. Even the traditional system of pounds and feet, although it works fairly well, still represents in our cultural memory the yoke of British domination thrown off 24 decades ago.

In fact, there has been an informal American system of weights and measures already in existence for generations. It has never been written down, but we all use it. Forget yards, acres, quarts, and gallons, not to mention hectares, meters and liters. Real Americans use bunches, paces, dashes, dabs, dollops, and handfuls (yes, handfuls not handsful). Miles are okay, but you never hear anyone say, "A miss is as good as a kilometer," and nothing says it better than "two hoots and a holler," "a stone's throw," or "about a driver and a nine iron."

There are signs our government will soon recognize this situation officially. According to a reliable source speaking on condition of anonymity, the Government Printing Office has stockpiled copies of a new consumer pamphlet designed to help everyone make better and more consistent use of this simpler, if less precise, system of weights, measures, and standards that is more compatible with the American character. Our source was able to snap a few pages with her iPhone so that we can share the information with you now.

CONSUMER'S GUIDE TO AMERICAN
WEIGHTS AND MEASURES
Abridged Edition

Office of Weights and Measures
National Institute of Standards and Technology
(Formerly the National Bureau of Standards)
US Department of Commerce

If you are confused by official US weights and measures or worried about understanding the metric system, this pamphlet will help. It explains commonly heard American terms. This Abridged Edition includes the most basic and a smattering of variations, mostly Southern.

For the more inclusive and politically correct Exhaustive Unabridged Edition covering Southwest, Northeast, Midwest, West Coast, Hispanic, Jewish, African American, Presbyterian, Texas, Cleveland and other variations, go to: www.consumersguidetoamericanweightsandmeasuresinclusiveexha ustiveunabridgededition.gov

You may use this pamphlet if you wish. Or don't use it. Whatever.

Capacity Measure
Here are a few common dry and liquid measures. Some are interchangeable for either dry or liquid, and some can be used for mushy stuff that isn't really either dry or liquid.

Trace	Dab	Tad	A lot	Skosh
Drop	Dash	Cup	Quite a lot	Too Much
Pinch	Dollop	Handful	Smidgen	Some

Relationships between these measures are subject to various interpretations to meet local conditions. Therefore, the following explanation is offered only as a guide:

Since a trace cannot be measured, the pinch is used as the basic unit. A smidgen is generally about two or three pinches. A dash is a couple of dabs, and a bit is about the same but a little more, while a dollop is a couple of good sized dashes. A handful is several dollops. A cup is a cup. A lot is obviously substantially more than a cup, at least a couple of them, and quite a lot is a lot more than that. A tremendous amount is almost more than you know what to do with, and a skosh more than that is really too much.

There are no conversion tables to show how these measures compare to any official system because everybody just knows this already.

Linear Measure

Close	Long ways	Two hoots and a holler
Pretty near	Hop, skip, and jump	Country mile
Step, pace	Stone's throw	Smack dab (in the middle)
Little ways	Far	Knee high to a grasshopper

Time

The international system of seconds, minutes and hours based arbitrarily on the number sixty doesn't make any sense. Although precise, these measures are more often expressed as approximate times, as in "just a second," "just a minute," or "about an hour." You may wish to practice these other terms as well:

Immediately	Soon	Recently
Right away	When ready	When I get around to it
As soon as possible	Next week	Sooner or later
In a jiffy	Late	Age, ages
Early	Lately	Never

Weights

A little	Light as a feather	Heavy
A lot	Lighter than air	Soaking wet
Light	A ton	About right

Quantity
These are helpful for counting things without having to use a bunch of confusing numbers.

A (one)	Few	Oodles	A lot
A couple	Quite a few	Many	More or less
Hardly any	Bunch	Too many	A whole lot
Some	Scads	Too much	Boatload

Fractions
Often these can be modified with words like large, small, thick, thin, etc.

Whole	Slice	Empty
Part	Helping	Rounded
Half	Pat	Level
Piece	Full	Heaping

Hard to Classify, but Helpful other Adjectives, Adverbs and Prepositions

Never mind if you don't know much about adjectives, adverbs, prepositions, and stuff like that.

Tiny	Rare	Just right	Good sized
About	Medium	Done	Bad
Pretty	Well	Hot	Gosh aplenty
Fairly	Soft	Cold	Smooth
Tender	Hard	Sort of	Crunchy

Practical Uses of the Information: Cooking

It's easy to see how all this can be helpful in many areas of daily life. Cooking, for example. Here are the recipes for some popular American dishes you may have hesitated to prepare because they seemed, like, too complicated in your standard cookbook. See if they aren't a whole lot easier now. Before starting, you might find these serving suggestions useful:

Helping	Spoonful	Ladle	Spread	Sprinkle
Plateful	To taste	Spoon	Pour	Drizzle
Glassful	Dole	Drop	Dump	Portion

Chocolate Chip Cookies

A couple handfuls shortening
A couple handfuls butter or margarine, softened
A cup granulated sugar
A cup brown sugar (packed)
A couple eggs
A couple dollops vanilla

A lot of all-purpose flour
Dollop soda
Dash salt
A cup chopped nuts
Quite a few semi-sweet chocolate pieces

Mix up the shortening, butter, sugars, eggs, and vanilla in a good sized bowl. Then add the rest of the stuff and stir some more. For softer cookies, add another handful of flour. Roll dough into small balls that look about the right size, and drop them onto an ungreased baking sheet a few fingers apart. Bake in a real hot oven until done. Cool slightly before removing from baking sheet.

Yield: A whole bunch of cookies.

Punch
Large canful pineapple juice, chilled
Large canful orange or grapefruit juice, chilled
A couple medium bottlefuls carbonated lemon-lime beverage, chilled
A couple medium bottlefuls ginger ale, chilled
A lot of lemon, lime, or raspberry sherbet
Quite a few slices lemons, limes, and oranges, fairly thin
Some mint leaves

Mix all the juices and carbonated beverages together in a pretty big punch bowl. Spoon sherbet into bowl. Drop in the fruit slices from not too high. Serve like right away.

If desired, a few dollops to a lot of wine or liquor of your choice can be added, as well as some ice cubes.

Yield: Quite a lot of punch (alternately, a bunch of punch)

Grilled Cheese Sandwich
A couple slices bread, pretty near any kind
A couple slices American cheese
Several pats butter, not too thick

Put the cheese between the slices of bread. Spread the butter on the outside surfaces of the bread without making too big a mess. Fry like a pancake in an ungreased skillet, turning the sandwich over until the cheese is melted and both sides look toasted and greasy, or broil in a hot oven on an ungreased baking sheet, maybe with some aluminum foil over it, watching it until it looks about right so it won't burn.

Yield: A sandwich

Soup
A lot of several kinds of vegetables
A lot of some kind of meat, but not as much as the vegetables
Dollop salt
Pinches and dashes of some other spices and herbs, to taste
A couple sprigs parsley
A whole lot of water

Chop up the meat and vegetables. Put these and all other ingredients except the water into a large cooking pot. Add the water. Heat to boiling, then reduce heat and let simmer for a while until the vegetables are soft enough. Add a skosh more of some of the seasonings if desired, until it tastes about right. Skim off any funny looking stuff.

Yield: A tremendous amount of soup

Stew

Same as soup, except let it simmer too long.

The Weights and Measures Word Game

Here's a challenging word game that's fun for the whole family!

We've taken a bunch of terms from the Exhaustive Unabridged Edition and mixed them up below. Your job is to figure out which category each of them belongs in. Is it dry measure, liquid measure, distance, weight, volume, or what? You decide. Extra points for words that belong in more than one category!

Glimmer, squirt, squeeze, hair, touch, lick, suspicion, tad, tad bit, mouthful, right much, mite, milli-fricker, awful lot, whopping, family size, institutional size, a whole lot, heap, whopping, right near, right here, right there, yesterday (sooner than immediately), finger, leap, bound, far and away, from here to there, yonder, city block, far piece, head and shoulders, from here to Eternity, right away, now, right now, in a sec (minute, hour [or so]), awhile, a while, last week, whenever, eventually, canful, mushy, dry, liquid, mashed, smidge, since when, coon's age, eons, occasionally, often, frequently, before you can say Jack Robinson, teeny-tiny, itsy-bitsy, teeny-weenie, teensy, teensy-weensy, tee-niney, several, very (big, small, early, late, etc.), real (big, etc.), right (big, etc.), never, loaded, garnish, smattering, soaking wet, more than, less than, very few, right few, any, so many, mass, flock, pile, passel, mess ("a mess o' ..."), right many, right much, gobs, medium, medium rare, more or less, hot, lump, jumbo, this close (space between index finger and thumb), extra, slightly, heaping, gubernatorial (not a weight or measure; we just like the word), packed, tremendous amount, almost, put a fork in it, stuffed, more, less, ready, lukewarm, chilly, chilled, right (small, big, etc.), bottleful, hint, taste, soupçon (oops, too French), whiff, shy of, mite shy of, fairly, just right, type of, as, industrial strength, huge, good, perfect, warm (close), hot (very close), cold (not so close), enough, not enough, ample, great deal, tinge, kindly, kind of, like, lacking, gosh aplenty, more than enough, super.

Good luck!

Smoke

A mirror on a wall in DC's White House,
a looking glass from Oxford's Christ Church hall.
Both see the world around for good and all,
yet comprehend no more than does a church mouse
which scenes reflected there are false or real
or slyly sprung from vain imaginations
going forth to seal the fate of men and nations,
throwing over common sense for guise and feel.
No matter how each episode's rehearsed,
how sleight the hand for mixing fact with fiction,
the mirror tells its tale of contradiction
that's never upside down but is reversed.
Such insight is a warning for us all,
exposing pride that goes before a fall.

Bob from BEP

The jetliner had been sitting on the airport tarmac since sundown, or about four hours, when I approached it on foot, dodging puddles from a passing thunderstorm. I had gotten there as soon as I could after receiving an encrypted call while wrapping up another case. I signaled the pilot to open the cockpit window, and when he did I flashed my badge.

"I'm from BEP," I shouted, hoping he could hear me over the drone of his idling engines. The rain had slacked off, so at least neither of us was getting wet. "Just call me Bob."

"I was sort of hoping it was you," said the pilot.

I could smell it now, wafting down from the cockpit window, even over the jet fumes and the steam from the wet tarmac. The characteristic aroma of overflowing toilets, sweat, dirty diapers, and mounting desperation. I thought I could hear shouting from behind the pilot, but it was probably just my imagination. Even so, I could picture the scene in the passenger cabin.

"How much longer do you plan on staying out here, Captain?"

"I'm not sure, sir. Air Traffic Control says the stormy weather in Memphis hasn't moved, and they won't clear me for takeoff."

"Why haven't you turned around and gone back to the terminal?" Of course, I knew the answer before I heard it.

"We were the last flight out, and when we left the gate the gate personnel and TSA security people all went home. I can't discharge and re-board passengers without security present," he said. "FAA regulations."

"How many terrorists do you think you have on your aircraft, Captain?"

He thought for a moment. "Well, I guess none, since everybody was cleared before they boarded."

"And if TSA made a mistake, do you think they'd somehow catch it when you let everybody back into the terminal to go to the bathroom?"

"No, sir."

"So the TSA people you say you need couldn't be counted on even if they were here, right?"

"Well, I guess not," said the captain, managing a weak smile.

"Yeah, I guess not either. But I will say, if you didn't have any terrorists when you left the gate, by now you probably have some folks who are thinking about it."

His Adam's apple bobbed as he gulped this down.

"Captain, I want you to turn this aircraft around now and go back to the terminal and discharge every passenger who wants to get off. You and your crew can operate the Jetway yourselves and do whatever you can to make everybody comfortable. Unload the baggage for those who don't want to re-board. Open up the café and cook hamburgers for everybody if you have to, and make sure everybody who still wants to go to Memphis gets there, on any airline, even if you have to wake up your boss and have him make the arrangements personally! You got that?"

He got it. Immediately the engines throttled up and the aircraft began to move.

"Will do, sir," he said with a little salute as he shut the window. "And thanks … Bob!"

To the imagined sound of cheering from the plane, punctuated by a bolt of lightning as the rain started again, I ran back to my black Lincoln Navigator and drove to the safe house. It was just another day at the office for Bob from BEP, the Bureau of Emergency Prevention.

That's the official name. It sounds lofty and well-meaning to political wonks who have no idea what we do, but we prefer the more descriptive Bull Extermination Patrol. Created during the Reagan years, we're the secret government agency charged with fixing stupid stuff the government does.

We rescue people from the unintended consequences of laws that weren't thought through before they were passed. We look for what we call "bull situations" (or "BS"), and then we do something about them.

The media don't know about us because mostly they don't recognize real BS anyway. But somehow word gets around to people who truly need to know. That pilot knew.

Some of you may think we're not doing a good job, but believe me, things would be much worse if we weren't here. We can't publicize our successes since we work outside the system doing things that are technically illegal—like ignoring an FAA regulation when it's clearly stupid not to. It's great when the BS itself gets publicity, but we don't want any for the agency. Until now.

Our agents come from all walks of life. Bill, the Director, is a former night club comedian who woke up one day and realized if the jokes he was telling about Washington were true (and mostly they were) then he really wanted to do something more about it than collect tips in a Mason jar. He took a CIA preparatory course and also made himself valuable on Reagan's campaign trail. That and his highly developed sense of the absurd positioned him for the job of starting the new agency.

Me, I was a cop in California until I caught a murderer in the act, smoking gun and everything. When they let him go on a technicality I turned in my shield.

BEP headquarters are in a Washington suburb, with offices in a storage shed at a landscape nursery we run as a front. That was Bill's idea—get a place that sells a lot of manure.

Our highly sophisticated bull detector technology works like this: When people run into frustrating government stupidity, they tend to say things like, "This is bull!" or "This is crazy!" or variations I won't mention. They communicate these expressions on cell phones and Internet social media. We monitor all those channels, and when a key expression is detected the software pinpoints the source and evaluates the situation based on message context. So if somebody says, "That's nutty!" it checks to make sure he's not just describing a candy bar.

When there is a verified BS, a call goes out to the nearest agent. That's how we heard about the jetliner. Many passengers used the key phrases on their cell phones, and our listening devices picked them up.

My partner, Jim, has his BS stories too. A favorite is about a HUD subsidized retirement community holding religious services in the common area. This violated the Fair Housing Act, according to the one resident who complained. We picked up lots of "This is bull!" messages from the other residents when the services were cancelled. Jim met with the facility manager.

"Now tell me again what Mr Williams says."

"He says he is an atheist and he's offended by the religious services even though he's not required to attend them," said the manager.

"So in other words," prodded Jim, "he thinks it violates his First Amendment rights?"

"Well, he *says* that, but I think he really just wants to watch the big screen TV in the common room where the services are going on. He complains on Bingo night too."

"Too bad Bingo isn't a religion."

"Around here it practically is."

"Okay," said Jim, "what you're going to do is announce that the Saturday and Sunday morning services will be resumed and that an atheist service will be held on Sunday afternoons."

"But how …?"

"Just do it. You invite the rabbi and the minister back, and BEP will supply somebody qualified to lead the other service."

"There are ordained atheists?"

"Maybe, but don't worry. In this case I'll lead the atheist service myself."

"You must be kidding," said the manager.

"'No religion left behind,' that's our motto at BEP," said Jim.

"Now you're mocking me."

"Listen," said Jim, "Mr Williams has a right to be an atheist, if that's what he is, but not to impose on the rights of others by hiding behind a stupid interpretation of a law. You make that announcement and I'll bet you won't hear anything more from Williams."

The manager caved. And Jim was right about Williams. Shortly after that, HUD made it official that public housing facilities can allow religious activities in the common areas.

Sometimes we get involved at the local level too. I think of Alan, jumping in when the New York City Health Department stopped a cigar shop from letting customers make their own coffee, for free, while they smoked the shop's cigars, a practice that had been going on for years. The shop didn't have a food-service permit. Smoking is banned in New York food-service establishments so if they had a food-service permit then no more smoking would be allowed in the cigar shop. The BS rallying cries were many and furious. It was a classic Catch-22 situation, the kind petty bureaucrats love. Or it was until Alan reminded the Health Department inspectors that the state law defines a food-service establishment as one that *sells* food, not one that gives it away free, and asked them if coffee was available in their offices and if so, whether they had a food-service permit. The inspectors withdrew quietly.

My next assignment would have been to go find out why a six year old girl in Ohio is on the Homeland Security "No Fly" list.

I'm getting to why I'm talking about this, even though it's secret. It may sound like fun and games, but believe me, it's not. BS can be tricky and dangerous. There are forces against us that go way beyond the anger of people we've embarrassed (although many are relieved when we show up because deep down they know they are doing something dumb). Political correctness has its own religious fanaticism, much stronger than atheism, or even Bingo, and common sense goes right out the window.

We all know the risks when we sign up. We've always known the only thing that could stop us would be another secret agency that would have to "neutralize" us quietly. We've never thought it would really happen, but for a while now I've had a feeling something *is* happening. Bill shared the same feeling during my last visit to headquarters. Now some of our agents have gone missing. And I'm in grave danger myself.

Last night at the safe house, during a thunderstorm, there was a knock on the door. Jim was in San Diego on a case, and anyway he wouldn't knock since he knows the keypad code. Still, I admit I let my guard down even though I knew it wasn't a pizza delivery because, after all, this was the safe house. I opened the door and a man about twice my size but dressed a lot like me pushed his way in out of the rain.

"Hello, I'm Bob," he said, dripping on the carpet.

"Well, I'm Bob too," I said, a little too brightly, as it turned out. I just assumed he was one of us in some kind of a jam and needed to get to the safe house in a hurry, without making the customary prior arrangements.

"Yes, I know," he said. "But I'm Bob from CURBEP."

"You mean …?"

"Yes, the Commission to Usurp and Remove the Bureau of Emergency Prevention. The Bull Extermination Patrol is going out of business. You're coming with me."

I had left my Taser in the kitchen, and given the mismatch in our sizes there was nothing I could do. He marched me out to a black Lincoln Navigator (not mine), threw me in the back seat, and made me put on a hood so I couldn't see. Then we drove for a long time. He only spoke to me once during the ride. "I'm really doing you a favor, you know. There's a wave of BS coming, the likes of which you've never seen, at least not in this country. Trust me—you don't want to be around for it!"

I didn't thank him.

Now here I am, locked in a small room with a toilet and no windows, somewhere. He didn't take my phone, but my calls just go to voicemail. When I text Jim or Bill, or any other agents, I never get a reply. My e-mails get Delivery Failure notices. Now I'm dictating this in hopes of leaving a record of what's happening, so our work won't be forgotten. The battery is low. The charger is back in the safe house, next to the Taser. I'm hungry. I've tried to call out on the phone and just say, "This is bull!" but I have a feeling nobody is listening anymore.

Sent from my Verizon Wireless 4G LTE Smartphone

189

Small Talk

Small talk
Smart way of greeting
Small talk
A party or a meeting
Small talk
Weighty as a feather
Itty bitty stuff
How 'bout this weather?

Small talk
Popular convention
Small talk
Heavenly invention?
Small talk
Not much to it
The devil's tool
and we all do it

Harmless enough
Never callous or rough
and never touches anything really tough

It's just small talk
Little words and sentences
Small talk
Helps to pass the time
Small talk
Tell me all your preferences
I'll look like I'm attentive
then pretend to tell you mine

Merry Christmas, Happy Hanukah
Blow a kiss to Aunt Veronica
Sister plays harmonica
Nothing rhymes with orange

Small talk
Real small talk

Getting to know you
Getting to know nothing about you
Getting to know you
and getting to hope you don't know me
Y'all come back now, y'hear?

But it's big talk
gives you some clout
Big talk
what it's all about
Big talk
makes the world go 'round
and political correctness
amplifies the sound

Without big talk
the world may cease to function
Big talk
Disease and mass destruction
Big talk
Gurus and politicians
Don't praise the Lord
but pass the ammunition

Wars are fought
for ideas and thought
and never mind the lessons our history's taught

When there's big talk
kings rise and fall
Big talk
Posture and brag
Big talk
Small seems tall
It's just small talk
in a bigger bag

The American People, fed up with disunity,
call upon the Black Hispanic Jewish Gay Muslim Asian Feminist Pro
Choice Pro Life Global Warming Gun Lobby One Percent
Nearsighted Senior Native American Presbyterian Community:*

Cut the big talk

But here's the big surprise
I'm starting to think
they give the Nobel Prize for
small talk
Very small talk

How 'bout them Redskins??

* For a complete list including the latest PC manifestos, creeds, talking points and
behavior guidelines, download the new Inclusiveness App for your iPhone, iPad,
Android or other device from the iTunes or Google Play Store.

The Ballad of Old John Smith

All the records were lost in the Flood 'O Forty-Seven, so
He'll never know now on this side of Heaven,
honest and true the real name he was given,
the man they just call Old John Smith.

Well, he can't hold a job 'cause he ain't got a ref'rence,
no documents, Green Card, ID, or a license.
Bosses these days got a definite pref'rence
for workers that ain't called John Smith.

Chorus
Singin', Who are you? Who are you?
Everyone thinks that your name is just a myth,
and you're fooling nobody but you,
Old John Smith.

The criminal background checks all come up empty,
yet still he's a man who just can't get no symp'thy:
"Get out of town or you'll stay here quite lengthy,
'cause we'll lock you up, Old John Smith."

Now when he says his name everybody starts groaning.
The obvious alias they're not condoning.
Such a lame name that he should be disowning,
to pick one that's not "Old John Smith."

Oh, he must have had parents before the disaster, and
maybe they're Murphy, O'Shea or Lancaster.
Poor John will die with no kin or ancestor, the
man they just call Old John Smith.

Chorus (x 2) *"Tell me, who ..."*

Coda
Fare thee well, Old John Smith,
fare thee well and gone.
Fare thee well, Old John Smith.
Take your name along.
Fare thee well, Old John Smith,
Johnny, we hardly knew ye.

Poor little Johnny boy ...
Didn't know who you were.

The County Library

(Originally published in the Writers' Group of the Triad poetry
anthology, *Fire & Chocolate*, January 2012. "Grammer" and
"pronounciation" are intentionally misspelled.)

I found a place you've gotta see,
down in the valley 'bout a mile from me.
It's called the County Library,
and you can take home books for free!
Yeah, you can take home books for free
down at the County Library!

There's books and magazines galore
on the shelves and on the floor.
There's comfy chairs and a whole lot more,
and you can smoke outside the door.
There's books on tape and DVDs
down at the County Library.

The ladies at the desk are nice,
but mind your manners is my advice.
Too much noise will sure suffice
to throw you out like you got lice.
So don't annoy the powers that be,
down at the County Library.

Check out all those books for free,
but you gotta bring them back, you see.
Forgot one time so I stood in line;
but all they said was, "That's a fine!"
Well if it's fine with them, it's fine with me,
down at the County Library.

Browse the Internet; there's no fee.
Look for a job or buy a TV.
There's no telling what you'll see,
but the racy sites are blocked (whew-ee),
so it's safe for the kids and the family,
down at the County Library.

Out back they've got a Book-Mobile.
It used to be a real big deal.
They say it lost its curb appeal, but
the whole idea's so surreal:
There's books with wheels? Well glory be!
Down at the County Library.

They hired a man with a funny name;
they lose a book, he gets the blame.
Like to meet him, but he can't be found;
Old' Dewey Decimal's not around.
He's hiding systematically,
down at the County Library.

Well, there's Borders, and Walden, and Amazon,
Barnes, and Noble, and Books dot com,
Target, and Walmart, and even eBay.
Only thing is … You gotta pay!
Don't need a literary shopping spree
when you can get your books for free,
down at the County Library.

Starbucks has its points I guess,
but it's sure not cheap, and it's not the best.
Hot water from the Men's Room – free –
makes my coffee, instantly.
And, well, that's good enough for me,
down at the County Library.

Can't use my cell phone, that's no go.
Disturbs the other folks, you know.
So leave a message at the beep and
here's a promise I might keep:
Call you soon as I am free
when I get home from the Library.

Learn new words, impress your friends.
They'll think you've been to school again.
So flaunt your tax-paid education,
grammer and pronounciation,
Like you got a P H Dee,
down at the County Library.

Now when I quit this mortal zoo –
check out before I'm overdue –
don't picture me in death's embrace …
Just put a bookmark in my place,
down at the County Library.
Down at the County Library.

Check it out!

I Gotta be You

I would be you. Where to begin?
Start with your passwords and your PIN.
Not too hard to get your credit cards,
your user IDs and your SSN.
It's easier than I thought.

Keys in your car, no need to guess,
got your home address from the GPS.
No ADT to worry me
and the car provides garage access.
Just one click and I'm in.

I'll search your papers where I'll find
a trove of the financial kind.
Ahh, bank accounts with fat amounts
for me, the criminal mastermind.
And extra checks. How nice!

Feet up on your furniture,
I'll bone up on your signature.
Ordered pizza with your Visa –
Extra toppings, that's for sure!
It's my house after all.

Hack your laptop? That's child's play,
using tips from the NSA.
(And one fine day I'll steal away
your fingerprints and DNA.)
Let the shopping spree begin.

Identity theft –
Gonna take your name.
Identity theft –
Got yourself to blame.
It's not my fault unless I get caught –
You left yourself open to my assault.

Identity theft –
Who's the one bereft?
Like you died, but I went to Heaven.

Deface of Fortune

Look at this nickel I found in the parking lot.
It's scratched almost beyond recognition from being run over so many times,
but see, right here, it looks like there's a design of some kind in the scratches.

Can you see it?

You're nodding.

Wow, maybe I've got something here.
Remember when somebody found Mother Teresa on a cinnamon bun?
Jesus on a rock?
The Virgin Mary on a grilled cheese sandwich,
a potato shaped like Ronald Reagan,
a peanut shaped like Jimmy Carter?

What do you think?
Maybe I can put it on YouTube and it'll go viral,
or sell it on eBay for a ton of money.
And what about Guinness?

I think it looks a lot like Thomas Jefferson, don't you?

Oh wait. It is Thomas Jefferson.

Dr Watson Calls 911

Holmes:
Hurry, Watson, there's no time to waste!
The game's afoot! Ring 911! Make haste!
Distressing machination
wants a rescue operation
lest the victim's life be dreadfully erased!

Watson:
Medical assistance, if you please,
to foil a threat more horrid than disease.
A grievous laceration
during self-defenestration
has my patient fast expiring by degrees.

Operator:
911. What's your emergency?
In smaller words please spell it out for me:
Your name and your location,
and the patient's situation.
After that, I'll send a team of EMTs.

Watson:
Pay no mind; it's now become too late
to save him from an essence-draining fate.
Unwarranted libation,
An extreme exsanguination,
all my ministrations failing in the wait.

Moral:
Cry of desperation, although brief,
in language erudite beyond belief:
Pedantic explanation
void of disambiguation,
causing utter deprivation of relief.

(In the UK the number is 999, but most American readers will not know that, so we'll pretend this takes place in the US and the 911 operator is befuddled by Watson's English accent. Two countries separated by a common language and all that.)

Round-Robin

A plethora of writers disagreeing on a story line

Round-Robin
A short story writing exercise gone wrong

For the information of you who have never attended a creative writing class, which I'm assuming is most of you, there is a favorite exercise called a "round-robin" wherein teams of four or five people, sometimes more, are formed and one person is assigned to write the first chapter of a short story starting with an opening sentence supplied by the instructor. For example, "There we were, sitting around the campfire eating our typical cowboy supper of sheep dip, buffalo chips and scalding coffee, when the sun finished its monotonous descent, bounced once, and disappeared below the western horizon." Person Number One writes the first chapter and e-mails it to Person Number Two who writes a second chapter and e-mails it to Person Number Three, and so on, until the last person writes the completion to the story.

If you ever have the opportunity to play this game, I recommend you volunteer to be Person Number One. Failing that, or if you are not the kind who can take off on just about any idea thrown at you or are shy about your writing skills, then you want to be the Last Person, the one who completes the story using all the presumably Good Stuff the other Persons have given you to work with. To be any Person in between is to waste your time, since you will have very little original to add without breaking the few "rules" of the exercise (see next paragraph), and anything good you actually do come up with will be completely missed, ignored, or totally unappreciated by the Persons who follow you and will end up not having contributed anything of value to the final story.

There are no rules other than the common sense idea that somehow there should be a plot, or at least a common thread woven throughout the story to make it hang together. A trace of character development is also looked upon with favor. But even these ideals can be cast aside if need be For the Sake of Art, although the instructor won't be amused. Someday I want to meet this "Art," for the sake of whom so much is done.

Until then, however, let's read an example of such an exercise. The team of writers in this case is larger than the usual four or five. In fact, I have lost count. Maybe it's 10 since that's how many chapters there seem to be, unless somebody with a big ego wrote more than one. Nor do I remember their names or genders, i.e., how many women, how many men, how many undeclared. See if you can figure it out. I do know Art got a pretty good workout here, his name being used in vain a bunch.

I'm the Last Person. The clean-up writer. I've had to edit the other chapters for grammar, spelling and punctuation, and I've inserted editorial comments here and there which I'm sure you'll be able to identify.

By the way, it occurs to me that if this guy Art is Japanese, then his Sake is rice wine. Not a bad prize to covet if there's enough of it and some beer to chase it with, but I know from experience it is an acquired taste.

Now here comes Chapter One.

CHAPTER ONE

There we were, sitting around the campfire eating our typical cowboy supper of sheep dip, buffalo chips and scalding coffee, when the sun finished its monotonous descent, bounced once, and disappeared below the western horizon. Everyone was nice to Clyde, even though he was the village idiot. After all, he had a tradition to uphold. His father and his grandfather and his grandfather's father before him had been village idiots, all named Clyde although not all in the same village.

In fact, great-grandfather Clyde the First was a sort of circuit idiot and went from village to village as he was needed.

Clyde was a humble man, and although he was also the regional mumblety-peg champion, he knew his place. However, he wasn't along with us this trip, which was pretty tough for the rest of us when we had to sit around night after night being nice to each other instead of having Clyde to take things out on. Jake spat and fell asleep on the campfire, spilling buffalo chips all over the place, but we acted fast so none of them would get burned.

Suddenly, Ray Charlie-Horse, our Indian Scout, got down on his knees, jabbed his knife in the ground, put his mouth over the handle, gritted his teeth, assumed a listening attitude, and barfed. It was an old Indian trick for determining the whereabouts of buffalo, and that clever old Charlie-Horse never did it the same way twice. Always an innovation on the old technique … like sometimes he would grab somebody else and shove *his* mouth over the filthy old knife handle. That's probably where he got the idea for barfing, since that's what everybody else always did.

"Sahib! Sahib!" he yelled as I unwrapped and hid his turban so the other men wouldn't get any funny ideas about what the heck kind of Indian Charlie-Horse was. "There are buffalo within fifty feet."

The Old Scout always came through for us when the chips were down even though he sometimes had trouble digesting his food, in which case the chips were up, and usually all over his sleeping bag. He barfed a lot, Charlie-Horse did. But this time the buffalo apparently didn't hear his warning shout, which would normally have caused them to stampede according to The Code of the West, so we were safe for the night.

Morning came in time for me to count and see how many of us were left. There were.

We all mounted up and rode on apiece until we came to a fork in the trail, which of course we took. After we rode on some more, our quarry came in sight. Jake was the first to throw off his clothes and jump in. We all followed, enjoying a welcome bath after four days in the saddle, even though the quarry meant we had taken the wrong turn back at the fork (Jake's doing, I'm sure) and would waste valuable time getting back on the right trail. But we needed a break, so we rested for an hour before pressing on. Jake fell asleep with his head in the crotch of a tree, probably dreaming of the village's pretty new schoolmarm, while Charlie-Horse went off to scratch his poison ivy in private. And barf if he felt like it.

I counted again, and by now there were only seven of us, but since I'm not so good at remembering names, I'm not sure who all it was. As a posse we left a lot to be desired. As Sheriff, I was embarrassed. Not only had I allowed Jake to mislead us at the fork, but also we were further slowed because Jake had brought his dog along. Normally Ole Blue was a good tracker, but Jake had failed to realize Ole Blue should've been called Ole Pink. This was a mistake I might have expected the idiot Clyde to make, but not Jake, unless Jake was thinking of vying for Clyde's job after Clyde went off to bigger and better things. If he ever did.

She gave birth to five puppies our fifth night out. That put us back another day. By now our real quarry, the dangerous Pork-in-the-Wall Gang, wanted for stealing the secret barbecue recipes of dozens of West Texas saloon keepers, nefariously substituting pork for beef and selling them on eBay, had no doubt passed out of our jurisdiction.

Plus, we had left our stinking badges back in town on the assumption we didn't need them.

I spent the next two evenings sitting around the campfire playing solitaire and hoping the Gang would double back in our direction. We had sent Ray Charlie-Horse on ahead to taunt them and then leave a trail of tantalizingly incomplete recipes leading back to our camp, where we planned to ambush them. It's not easy for one man to sit around a campfire, but I had on my stretchy leotards (from the days when I fancied myself a ballet dancer, but that's a story for another time), which made it easier until about 2:00 a.m. on the second night when the elastic snapped and there went the buffalo chips again.

And that's when we all heard the sound of approaching horses. The Gang was coming back. We had only moments to get ready. Clyde would have loved it.

Him being an idiot and all.

CHAPTER TWO

You may be wondering why Clyde wasn't with us on this trip. That's a story worth telling here because it will give the appearance of at least a common thread, if not a plot.

Clyde was running for Congress and was very busy with his campaign. This involved making speeches, knocking on doors, making promises, kissing babies, and eating lots of fried chicken and barbecue, both beef and pork, both of which he claimed to be his favorite, depending on his audience.

It had not been easy to convince Clyde to run for office. It happened this way. There we were, sitting around our usual table at the Hot Darn Saloon, just Clyde, Redondo Beech, Black Bart, and me, having a couple of beers and complaining about life in general, when Black Bart said, "You know, I'm just about fed up with them idiots in Washington."

"Oh yeah? Whyizzat, Black?" asked Redondo, pushing back a lock of sandy hair.

Black Bart's name really was Black Bart. His parents had named him Bart Black, which would have been written "Black, Bart" on his birth certificate, but somehow the recording clerk left out the comma, so Black Bart it was. He wore his hat backwards, and when there was a choice he entered buildings at exits and exited at entrances. He also ran the village newspaper, *The Village Newspaper*, having taken it over from his father, Grey Black, when the latter succumbed to liver failure. Black Bart had carried on the editorial tradition of his father, which meant the paper rarely carried any good news, and the editorials were diatribes against all authority, except mine of course, as Sheriff. The only letters to the editor that got published were those that agreed with him. No wonder our little village was down on itself all the time. Nobody had anything good to say about it, and worse nobody realized it was even possible to say anything good about our village, or any village, or about anything at all. Even more worse, Black was a poor speller and knew little about grammar.

"Oh, you know … all the burdensome regulations that slow down us small businessmen. The endless paperwork, taxation of everything that moves, giving women the right to vote! And now verification of citizenship. Shoot, I may be an illegal alien myself for all I know! But better'n bein' a Indian, I reckon."

"Let's hear it for Native Americans!" shouted Redondo to no one in particular. "A right worthless bunch if ever there was one!" Redondo had apparently partaken of some firewater before joining us at the table.

"That's no way to talk about Charlie-Horse behind his back," I said. "You know he always comes through when the chips are down."

"I say if we were born in this country, then we're all native

Americans," announced Clyde, who had been pretty quiet, almost disengaged, up to that point, although I noticed his eyes narrowed when Black mentioned Washington.

Black and Redondo looked at him as if he were an idiot.

Black cupped his chin in his hand. "Clyde, I think you've done give me a idear."

"Meaning what?" said Clyde.

"Meanin' you should run fer Congress, of course!"

"Oh no, I could never do that! I'm no politician."

"You don't have to be a politician, Clyde. Just be yourself."

"Yeah, let's send up a real idiot to show 'em how it should be done!" offered Redondo.

"Right," continued Black, "and with us and my newspaper behind you, you'll be a shoo-in!"

"I don't know …" protested Clyde. "I'd have to ask my grandpa."

"What, is he smarter 'n you all of a sudden?" Black shot back.

"Maybe not, but …"

"And besides, as regional mumblety-peg champion you already know how to perform in front of an audience. I'd say you're more 'n qualified to be a Congressman. What do the rest of you think?"

It was obvious Redondo was in favor of it, although I don't know that he fully understood the conversation. As far as I was concerned things couldn't get much worse in Washington, and Clyde might be a breath of fresh air. So sure, what the heck.

"It's settled then!" said Black. "Clyde, you just promise me you'll keep your nose clean up there and do whatever it takes to get the railroad to come through our village, and I'll run you the finest campaign you ever did see, and when you win I'll personally treat you to a big steak dinner right here."

"I do like steak."

Much later, Clyde came to me in private.

"I don't know where this is going, Sheriff," he said, "but it's been a learning experience hanging out with you guys."

"What do you mean?" I asked.

"Well, I was conflicted about this running for Congress thing, as you probably know. I realize I'll be up against a lot of competition in Washington. But I made a decision, and now I find myself on a quest. I feel like I'm experiencing character development. That's important, isn't it?"

"Yes, I think it is."

"And, you know, I bet there's more to come."

CHAPTER THREE

If I end this next chapter by revealing that what happened in it was just a dream, you will feel cheated. You will think I am a hack with no imagination, who has no idea what a plot is, or even a common thread. "Too convenient," you will say. "And what about the anachronisms?" you will also say. So let me say it clearly, right up front. It was a dream. Get over it.

Seven-thirty in the morning. I awoke, stretched, got out of bed, and looked in the window. It was still dark in my bedroom, and only now were the few weak rays of the rising sun beginning to pierce the gloom. I suppose I could have seen more if I had been able to open the blinds, but that wasn't going to happen. And it had been this way for the past three mornings, ever since I locked myself out of my apartment.

I had been sleeping on the sidewalk outside my window on a mattress generously loaned to me by my friend, Clyde, who lived in a nearby sewer. He didn't need the mattress because lately he had taken to wandering the streets at night in search of his grandfather and namesake, a former Congressman from Texas who had gone missing in the midst of scandalous allegations.

At first I couldn't believe I had locked myself out. I knew I had the key with me when I left the last time, but I must have lost it somewhere. The only answer was to retrace every step I had made since I last left the apartment and locked the door. The key had to be somewhere along that route. Now why hadn't I thought of that two days ago? Pooling my money, I started by hopping a passing streetcar and going to the zoo, which is as good a place as any to look for something. The animals were just as I remembered them … big and hairy and smelly. I went to the elephant house and looked around for a while but didn't find the key anywhere. On the way back to town I dropped a dollar bill down a sewer grating so Clyde could buy a candy bar or something. It was the least I could do.

About noon I stopped into a little restaurant for my usual lunch of two chicken, lettuce, and emu tongue club sandwiches and a cup of soup *du jour*. And there it was. "Waiter," I said with a couple of club sandwich toothpicks between my teeth, "there's a key in my soup *du jour*."

"I can't understand you, sir. You seem to have a mouth full of toothpicks."

I agreed that I did, and he in turn was forced to agree there was indeed a key there in the soup *du jour*. I stiffed the waiter his tip for talking back and took off for my apartment.

Shooing the pigeons away from the door, I stuck the key in the lock and went in.

Inside it was a different world. A bunch of little hairy nymph guys ran up and took off my trench coat for me while I was escorted in by a unicorn wearing an embroidered loincloth and a Caterpillar hat with a hole in it. For its horn. Over by the TV sat this roly-poly jerk who was mostly naked except for a big crown on his head. He was holding a pitchfork, but even as he introduced himself as King Neptune I remained suspicious.

213

"If you loonies don't clear out of my apartment I'm calling the cops!" I yelled, but this Neptune guy just smiled and kicked one of the little hairy nymphs who scuttled off to the bathroom and was back in a flash with the toilet seat and a tube of toothpaste, the kind that comes out of the tube looking like a peppermint candy cane noodle. Setting the toilet seat on the floor near the wall, he commanded me to sit on it and handed me the toothpaste.

Pointing first at my fingers and then at himself, Neptune said precisely, "You ... paint!"

This chapter is written in answer to all my friends who have undoubtedly wondered, but who have politely not asked, why I have toothpaste finger-painting on my wall that looks like a big naked jerk with a crown and a pitchfork. What the toilet seat had to do with anything is anybody's guess.

Now I can hear you saying, "Well, okay, maybe it was a dream after all. It's too bizarre, and he's not smart enough to have come up with that all on his own. And, wow, how about those anachronisms, eh?"

CHAPTER FOUR

They approached warily, four on horseback and one on foot leading his mount. I made sure my men were all in position. This would be the Pork-in-the-Wall Gang's last stand.

Ole Pink let out a low growl, but she was safely out of earshot in the lean-to, and we had hushed the puppies with, uh, hush puppies. Soaked in cheap whiskey.

Jake was positioned high up on a rock outcropping overlooking the trail but safely obscured by some scrub pine. He carried his old Winchester that had seen him through many a tight spot. Ray Charlie-Horse would circle back around the Gang and cover them from behind to cut off any escape. The rest were posted in other advantageous spots, all with rifles or scatterguns at the ready and pistols strapped to their thighs. That is, all but Black Bart. Acting as the imbedded reporter for *The Village Newspaper*, he would take notes.

The whole Gang was well covered. The action would start on my signal. The trouble was, we had forgotten to agree on a signal. Although it was now 2:30 a.m., it was a clear, moonlit night, so a hand signal would have been good, but since those can be confusing, it would have to be an audible one, which fortunately meant pretty near anything would do.

Hoping he wouldn't mistake it for a white flag of surrender, I stepped out into the clearing waving an incomplete barbecue recipe and stopped directly in front of Pork Wall, the Gang leader, startling his horse.

"This what you're looking for, Porky Pie?" I said sneeringly as the other Gang members surrounded me on their horses, sneering, their guns drawn.

"Could be," answered Pork sneeringly. "Depends."

Pork's horse had recovered and whinnied, but sneeringly.

"On what exactly?" I asked sneeringly.

"On if'n it's complete, o' course. Not like them fakes you and your boy Charlie-Horse a'been saltin' along the trail here 'n' there. Along with barf."

"Oh, it's complete all right," I said sneeringly. "Even includes directions for sauce and cole slaw. You'll love it. Should fetch a bundle on eBay!"

"Well, 'case you didn't notice, my boys has got you surrounded, so you might just as well hand it over now so's nobody'll git hurt. I know you got ole Ray hanging around somewheres, but the two of you ain't likely to take all five of us," Pork said sneeringly.

It was time to give the signal.

"Here's the signal, boys! Let's get 'em!"

215

Not very original, but it's all I could think of at the time. It seemed adequate. However, the other trouble was we had also forgotten to agree on what to do when I did give the signal.

There was a rustling of boots and chaps from overhead and behind the Gang, and they looked up and around to see a shower of incomplete barbecue recipes floating down at them, obscuring their view of me and spoiling their aim. My men rushed in, pulled the Gang off their horses and tied them up along with Pork before there was any gunplay.

"Good work, boys!" I shouted triumphantly.

"Got to admit, you fooled me this time, Sheriff," said Pork sneeringly, "but this ain't over yet. No, sir, not by a long shot."

But it was.

CHAPTER FOUR

Casablanca!

I walked into the bar and probably would have brained myself if one of the stools hadn't broken my fall. My dirty trench coat clung to my sides, dripping wet from the heavy fog which filled the streets.

"I must open my sealed orders at eleven," I thought to myself.

Then I spun around on my stool, and saw *her*. I didn't know *she* was going to be here. I wondered if *he* knew. Our eyes met with a flash of raw cornea, pupils dilating.

Somehow it didn't add up. Of all the gin joints, in all the towns, in all the world, she walks into mine … except it wasn't mine.

He knew. Emu.

Then Emu walked in. It was too much. I tried to keep from laughing. Laying a finger aside of my nose, I concentrated on cleaning out my mind of all the stagnant thoughts, the old prejudices of long ago, but they all came into perspective now. I hate Casablancans. And emus. Casablancan emus in particular.

While I was clearing my head she had left the room, but now she walked back in, her dress in disarray. Her breathing was heavy. She wanted to tell me something. I knew it. We all knew it. Even he knew it, but he didn't know he knew it … you know?

I mean I knew what she wanted to say, but I wasn't in the mood.

I cracked a new deck of Luckies, blew the tobacco into my drink, and finished it off. When I get nervous, nothing helps.

"I haven't got time for any of your 'cock and emu' stories," I said sneeringly. "I'm still trying to work out exactly what the anachronisms were in Chapter Three."

Besides, it was eleven, and I was opening my sealed orders.

CHAPTER FIVE

Emu had ethnic problems. We always thought he was too chicken to stick around and see how they came out, but the fact that he was chicken scared the dickens out of him. How would you feel if you were an emu who was a chicken? A chicken emu not only has ethnic problems but psychological problems as well. Emus despise chickens. So Emu left town one night in a fog, leaving nothing behind but his dirty, dripping wet trench coat which several of us drew lots for. (Wow! Two threads in the first paragraph alone! This is some writer!)

Clyde was the winner. (Three!) He always has been a lucky bird even though he is the village idiot. (Four! Be still, my heart!) Please let me know if any of you out there see or hear anything about Emu. He's a little smaller than an ostrich, and he has sort of sandy hair. He owes me money. On the other hand, he did lend me his mattress when I was in need. (Five!) Or was that Clyde?

So the next night, me and some of the boys are sitting around down at Al's doing a little finger painting when this broad comes in. I stand up and she passes me a finn which I can keep if I do a special sitting for her. Well of course I sit back down right away, but she grabs the five bucks back real quick and yells, "Get up, you!" Of course I haven't wiped off my hands yet and when I grab her trench coat to steady myself it makes this big mess with the finger paint. But she's cool. She means she wants me to paint her, not sit down. Great! So I look at her trench coat and since it looks like I've already done the job, I ask for my money again.

Just then a monkey runs down the bar and drops a cigar butt in my finger paint jar. But like I said, this broad is too cool, and she's got her trench coat off quicker than two shakes of a monkey's uncle and she's grabbed the monkey, stuffed him in the pocket, and is beating the coat as hard as she can against the bar, knocking over everybody's finger paint jars.

In a flash I'm at the bar and I slug this dame right in the mouth, catching my finn as she falls, and then she's flat out on the floor with a smile on her face. It's sort of a green and yellowish smile and it's smeared all over her face because I still haven't wiped my hands off yet.

Just then the monkey's uncle comes in.

CHAPTER SIX

The scene opens on a fish net with a couple of those old glass globes the Japanese used in the WW II era to make their nets float. Through the net can be seen a six-foot sailfish mounted on a wall plaque. To the left hangs a tattered old-fashioned map of the world showing the 17th Century conception of the American coastline, the route of Marco Polo, the wreck of the Hesperus, and the Rime of the Ancient Mariner. The camera pans to a ruddy faced UNCTUOUS ANNOUNCER sitting just under the map in a wicker chair pretending to adjust the azimuth of a Jivaro Indian blow gun he is pretending to aim at the cameraman. As the camera dollies in, the UNCTUOUS ANNOUNCER'S cheeks puff out briefly, and the camera suddenly shows a view of the studio ceiling, jumps once, and shows the same scene as before only now sideways. Stereotypical African adventure type music fades in. The scene goes right side up again.

UNCTUOUS ANNOUNCER: Once again we present the adult adventure drama, "Soldiers of Adventure." This is another in a series of dramas presented in the interest of promoting the intellectual theatre in America and supported by Viewers Like You. Thank you. Through your kind patronage we may make enough money off this show to start promoting that good old intellectual theatre very soon now. Art for Art's sake, as we all know. And we do want Art to have some nice threads to wear. And some sake.

Starring internationally acclaimed author, explorer and fortune hunter, Lance Durango, as himself and Craig Lister as "Squeamish" Ed Hildebrand, supported by an all-star cast, "Soldiers of Adventure" ranks as one of the true great jungle epidemics … er, epics.

As we join the latest episode, Lance and Ed are deep in the jungle of Tanzania with their native guide and trusted companion, Rudyard Charles. They are hot on the trail of a gang of diamond smugglers but have stopped at an abandoned Forest Ranger hut so Ed can rest. Lance is the first to speak.

LANCE: You know, Ed, I'm getting pretty darn tired of having to stop every 20 minutes at these abandoned Forest Ranger huts so you can rest!

(Ed, dressed in leotards [Ah, the real thread. I was wondering.] and combat boots, openly favors his very swollen left leg.)

ED: Well, confound it, Lance, this leg is heavy! And it's so swollen it's almost impossible to get my leotards on every morning. Was it my fault there was a banana peel on the fire escape at that hotel in

Mwanza? Although I must admit the barbecue they served was pretty good. I wonder what kind of meat they used. Didn't taste like pork or beef. I'll bet it was gazebo.

LANCE: Don't you mean gazelle?

ED: No, I'm pretty sure I mean gazebo.

LANCE: Ed, everybody knows a gazebo is a small open sided building in a park.

ED: Yeah, but if the plural is spelled "gazeboes" and not "gazebos" then it's an animal. It's closely related to the belvedere, the plural of which, of course, also happens to be "belvedere." Anyhow, I'd love to see the recipe.

LANCE: I'm still pretty sure it's a building.

ED: Funny thing is, it tasted like chicken. Besides, I wish you'd stop complaining every time we stop at one of these abandoned Forest Ranger huts! I'm sick of it! Sick, do you hear?? SICK!

(*Shot of big yellow fungus growth on nearby tree. Unpleasant sound is heard. New shot of Lance, wincing.*)

LANCE: Sorry, Ed. Guess I'm just jumpy, that's all. This assignment has me worried.

ED: Yeah, I notice even Rudyard here looks a little pale. Our nerves are all on edge, expecting something from … the unknown.

(Ten ferociously scarred and painted semi-nude tribal warriors run past the hut, five playing bagpipes and five dribbling basketballs.)

ED: Ask 'em if they know "Sweet Georgia Brown."

LANCE: Forget it! What's more important right now is, what are all these abandoned Forest Ranger huts doing here in Tanzania?

ED: I was wondering what became of all the abandoned Forest Rangers.

LANCE: That does it! Rudyard, hand me your machete!

RUDYARD: Yes, Bwana.

(Camera shifts away discretely to a scene of grazing emu. [Thread!] Sounds of heavy work with machete, accompanied by panting and grunts.)

ED: Lance, cut it out! Figuratively of course. What are you doing?

LANCE: There was a four-leaf clover over there. I told my little niece back in New Jersey I'd bring her a souvenir of Africa.

(Close up of Lance, emphasizing his basic wholesomeness. He lovingly puts the clover into his cigarette case which we see also contains a photo of a woman who is presumably his mother.)

ED: It's beyond me how one man can get so much pleasure out of emphasizing his basic wholesomeness all the time.

LANCE: You should try it sometime.

(*Once again the camera discretely shifts, this time to a shot of wild giraffes (or "giraffe") stampeding before an oncoming locomotive followed by a band of screaming Native Americans. The Native American chief raises his rifle and instantly the other Native Americans are on the ground with their knives firmly implanted in the soil and their mouths over the handles … barfing. Unfortunately, they become so wrapped up in this old Native American trick for determining the whereabouts of giraffe they are trampled by a herd of gazeboes entering from the left. Shift back to hut.*) [*So many threads here you could knit leotards!*]

LANCE: We'd better get started again if we hope to reach the village by nightfall. To be caught out here in the jungle at night …

(*Dynamic shot of an angry elephant hopping about, apparently having stubbed its toe on something*)

C'mon, Rudyard!

RUDYARD: Yes, Bwana.

(*Shot of native women bludgeoning their garments at the river bank in an effort to get them clean*)

LANCE: Look out! It's the ferocious Woobi-Goobi women! Quick! Hide! It's absolutely taboo for white men to see them doing their laundry! If we're caught they'll make us help!

(*While Lance and Ed hide, Rudyard barters with the Woobi-Goobi for their safety. Excited gestures are exchanged as Rudyard gives them trinkets from his laundry bag. Trinkets such as beads, tobacco, pantyhose, etc.)*

ED: That was close!

LANCE: We should reach our goal before nightfall if nothing else goes wrong!

RUDYARD: What you mean "we," white Bwana?

LANCE *(makes as if to slap Rudyard)*: You've been saying that just about every half hour, and it's not funny anymore!

RUDYARD: Peace Corps man not think so either.

ED: Lance?

LANCE: Yeah, Ed, what is it?

ED: Could we stop and rest a minute here? I'm getting tired.

LANCE: We might as well. It's eleven o'clock and time for me to open our sealed orders anyhow.

(Music comes up as the scene fades to the Unctuous Announcer.)

UNCTUOUS ANNOUNCER: And so we leave Lance Durango, and "Squeamish" Ed Hildebrand, and of course, Rudyard, hot on the trail of the diamond smugglers. Be on hand next time as we continue our exciting adventure story when we will hear Lance say:

223

LANCE: Rudyard, can you fly a B-27?

UNCTUOUS ANNOUNCER: That's in the next exciting episode of "Soldiers of Adventure."

(Music up as credits crawl across the screen. A small naked boy runs between the camera and the credits making an obscene gesture as the screen quickly goes black.)

CHAPTER EIGHT

A bunch of us sour grapes were sitting around the other night at the Lodge eating peaches, drinking scalding coffee, and making up poems to pass the time while waiting to become sour raisins. That's all very symbolic, of course, as well as a sneaky way of admitting that some of my friends and I enjoy making up poems for amusement. A couple of the guys were knitting too, as a matter of fact, but that is neither here nor there. Except there are threads involved.

The sun had just bounced below the western horizon, and I had shoved the aeolipile out of the way so I could stretch out a little more in my leotards, which had a habit of drawing me up into a shriveled little ball if I wasn't careful, when Iggy got up to recite. We'd been taking turns since about eight o'clock, and this was Iggy's seventh poem. However, he only managed to get the first three lines out:

"O horn of plenty, O Cornucopia, O tempura, O mores, O benefactor of the
downtrodden and lousy,
give me your tired, your poor, your huddled masses ..."

when he was overcome by one of his coughing spells and had to be helped back to his seat. It was just as well, as we were tiring of Iggy's vain attempts at the fusion of Irish imagery and Japanese food. But with no sake. Now it was Nate's turn.

Nate had come late again as usual. He had such a penchant for trite poetry that he always came late just so everyone would have to say, or at least think, "It's Nate and he's late," or some equally shallow variation thereof. There was no getting around it either. He also took similar advantage of his last name, which was Bass.

Nate had always had a flair for verses, and he was especially fond of writing them in public restroom stalls. Sometimes he would spend hours in a stall, which used to worry his parents when he was younger until they found out what he was doing. Anyway, this was the first time we'd heard a poem from Nate this evening. And you could tell right away he'd been working on this one for a long time. Here is as much of it as I could piece together this long after the event. I had to visit a lot of restroom stalls.

Lovely Ophelia, were I as steadfast as thou art.
Take pity; unload thine affections; make manifest thy manifold charms,
gath'ring my mimsy borogoves into your arms
with ever-open eyes whose light thine ossifying lids can ne'er extinguish,
beholding skin with scarce a multitude of blemish.
Thy modesty,
thy peach-like ears so wondrous soft,
thy lips which kiss no more the flowers of the morn too oft
mixed with poison ivy,
thus not rendering thy mouth
a travesty.
Hail, pale lover, why so wan?
Wan not?

What would I have thee beest?
Thy countenance bespeaks thou seest
far too well for mortal contemplation,
as gentle unto that dark knight of self-condemnation
th'art surely not a foul abomination.
Faint praise for rose by any other name,
the object of my love, Ophelia,
you, through rain, wind, sleet,
and snow, pale lover's hail to greet,
nor gloom of night, nor fame.
O playgirl of the Western World,
whose dappled ringlets festoon the balcony of thine heart,
be mine!

When Nate finished he was so wound up he accidentally tripped on the pile of peach pits. Then he got up and sprawled in a corner. The peach pits had been building up since we started having these sessions in February, and the pile was now about three feet high. Sort of a mess to fall on because the top ones were still wet and sticky.

Jake, who occasionally joined us when he wasn't spending time with his girlfriend, a pretty schoolteacher back in the village, spat into the pile and then fell asleep on the window sill. He never could eat more than a half dozen peaches before passing out.

I don't remember very well what happened between then and when I woke up in the hospital. They tell me Jake and I are the only survivors of an explosion and fire apparently started by spontaneous combustion in the peach pit pile.

I wish Clyde had been there. He would have loved it.

Him being an idiot and all.

CHAPTER NINE

The Conclusion

I couldn't believe it when I drew the short straw that meant now I have to be the one who writes the last chapter in this stupid story. I have to clean up the mess made by a bunch of arrogant hacks who think they are real writers who are above following even the simplest instructions on how to write a round-robin. Each one feels he or she needs to use his or her chapter to take the story off in some unique direction and the heck with whoever comes after. So I get all the heck. The hack heck.

But first, I'm opening my sealed orders. I don't care whether it's eleven o'clock or not because my leotards are too darn tight and the sooner I get on with this the sooner I can take them off, put on my jeans and tweed jacket with the leather elbow patches, slip into my Topsiders, grab my pipe and tobacco pouch, and run over to Starbucks, order some scalding coffee, and meet the other so-called writers for the story post-partum party.

They'll be eager to read this. Each will be smugly looking to see that his or her chapter set the tone for the rest of the story. All of them will be disappointed. They'll put a good face on it, of course, heartily congratulating one another for their contributions while wordlessly cursing me for not celebrating their singular talents and brilliance by making their chapter the centerpiece. Well, nuts to them all. I'm not Rudyard, and I could care less about making Bwana happy.

I did think Chapter One was competently written in spite of the inevitable clichés, and Chapter Two showed some promise, but whoever wrote Chapter Three took off on a weird tangent totally missing, or more likely deliberately ignoring, where the story could have gone. At least the writer of Chapter Four tried to get it back on some kind of consistent track, but after that the story, if you can call it that, went in more directions than a Fourth of July starburst, making a travesty of the whole exercise.

227

I'm referring to the first Chapter Four, since I notice there are two of them. Jerks! They can't write *and* they can't count.

Not only are there two Chapter Fours (or is it Chapters Four?), but also I notice there is no Chapter Seven. If it exists, that will mean there were 10 chapters altogether. I suppose the possibly mythical Chapter Seven will hereafter be known in local round-robin lore as "The Lost Episode." I hope it stays lost, but, no, it will probably turn up somewhere.

And whoever wrote Chapter Eight is an idiot. Even dumber than Clyde, who at least amounted to something in the end, as you will see.

It's getting late. The sun has finished its monotonous descent, bounced once, and disappeared below the western horizon. The sealed orders say I must be at the Starbucks rendezvous in less than an hour, so here's what I'm going to do. Instead of trying to wrap everything up neatly in a plot-resolving chapter that gives the good guys their rewards and the bad guys their comeuppances in surprising ways and satisfyingly ties up all the loose ends but with a twist, I'm just going to do one of those roundups like you see at the end of a lot of movies where little "what became of the main characters and where are they now?" statements crawl up the screen while the music plays. Ready? Here goes.

CLYDE did become a Congressman, running first as an independent but switching to the Libertarian party during his eighth and final term in the House of Representatives before being appointed Secretary of State, where he served with distinction, meaning he did almost nothing, until retirement. Later, he and a few well-connected friends from back home founded Senate House, Inc., a nonprofit retreat and training center for young, aspiring politicians, coining for it the now-famous slogan, "It takes a village to raise an idiot."

JAKE opened a pet kennel on the outskirts of the village, but he never could persuade Ole Pink to live with him there. It was as if she sensed, after the gender misidentification episode on the trail, that Jake had no idea what he was doing. The kennel struggled until it was closed down by the authorities after which Jake, never quite the same after the peach pits exploded, became a hermit, living by his wits and his trusty Winchester out in the wilderness.

RAY CHARLIE-HORSE choked on a knife handle as his trail companions looked on in helpless horror after discovering the instructions in their first aid kits for performing the Heimlich Maneuver were in German. Why he seemed to be trying to eat his knife is anybody's guess.

REDONDO BEECH went to work for Black Bart at *The Village Newspaper* after the Pork-in-the-Wall Gang was rounded up, correcting Black's spelling and grammar and encouraging the continuation of the paper's editorial negativity.

BLACK BART'S sympathetic newspaper coverage of the Pork-in-the-Wall Gang's exploits and eventual roundup, written from the criminals' point of view, earned him a Pulitzer Prize. Black used the $10,000 award to start a second, competing newspaper devoted to carrying only optimistic, good news stories. It was called *The Other Village Newspaper* and folded after six months, there being a general dearth of good news in the village, much less the world, despite Black's best efforts to make up as many stories as he could. Finally, still wearing his hat backwards, which made him look like he was coming and going at the same time, he was shot dead by a nearsighted, elderly security guard at the Walmart while trying to enter an emergency exit, setting off the alarm and causing the overzealous guard to think he was a shoplifter trying to sneak out.

THE SHERIFF made a name for himself (although he doesn't have one in the story) by masterminding the demise of the Pork-in-the-Wall Gang. That name was "The sheriff who masterminded the demise of the Pork-in-the-Wall Gang," or Tswmtdotp-i-t-wg for short. While responding to a call about a suspected shoplifting at the Walmart he was shot dead by the nearsighted, elderly security guard who mistook him for Black Bart's accomplice.

OLE PINK (née Ole Blue) lived out her days under the porch at the Hot Darn Saloon nursing a parade of pups in flagrant violation of the village's anti-littering ordinance.

THE PRETTY NEW SCHOOLMARM, after a brief romance with Jake, ending when she discovered he didn't know what he was doing, married a banker and lived in a house with indoor plumbing.

NEPTUNE, appearing in a dream, was therefore never really in the story. Whatever his main occupation, he also moonlighted as a planet. (Get it? *Moon*lighted … as a *planet*?)

THE PORK-IN-THE-WALL GANG hadn't actually broken any laws and was let off with a warning by the judge. Pork Wall and the Sheriff eventually became good friends and spent many an evening sitting around at the Hot Darn Saloon sneeringly re-telling their exploits for townsfolk and strangers alike, though they didn't cotton to strangers much, 'specially Pork, until the night the Sheriff didn't come back from the Walmart. Pork bought a barbecue recipe on eBay and opened a restaurant. It closed after three months because he didn't cotton to the customers, tending to address them sneeringly and preventing the waitresses from taking their orders if he didn't like their looks. He then took over the security duties at the Walmart but stayed away from the customers. The other Gang members enrolled in IT courses at the community college and became computer hackers.

EMU never did find himself, as far as we know, nor did anyone ever find him. He still owes me money. Or is that Clyde?

LANCE DURANGO (aka Bwana), "SQUEAMISH" ED HILDEBRAND, and RUDYARD never wanted to be in this story in the first place, and for all practical purposes they were not, even though the writer threw in some decent threads. What story they were actually in is anybody's guess, but I wish them well.

IGGY. Nobody cares about Iggy. Forget him.

NATE BASS, the sadly derivative poet, did survive the peach pit pile explosion in spite of initial reports, yet still managed to show up late for his own funeral, which was conducted by friends who thought he had died. He continued his career as an amateur wannabe poet, achieving some small notoriety. However, most of the poems he later became known for were rude limericks featuring his name and written by others.

Now I'm off to Starbucks. I'm not looking forward to it. Wish me well.

Ripped from the Headlines

Eat your heart out, William Randolph Hearst!

More Indigestion in Fast Food

A *Winnovation Magazine* Special Report
By Walt Pilcher, staff writer

Ten years ago, Morris Dunster was just one of hundreds of MBA students at the Harvard Business School. Like many of his classmates, he dreamed of becoming a successful entrepreneur. In what started as a project for a small business management class, Dunster and a team of three other students hit upon an idea for a chain of fast food restaurants that has since grown to become the multi-billion dollar operation known as Lone Ranger's.

The early days were rough. It took three years of hard work after graduation before Lone Ranger's sales and profits took off in full gallop. But now discouraging words are being heard and although skies are not yet cloudy all day, some investors are finding it difficult to see a silver lining.

All four original Harvard teammates are still with the company, and each gives the others credit for coming up with the idea for the business. "We knew it was crazy to even think about getting into fast food at that time," says Dunster from the company's headquarters just outside Lebanon, Kansas. "The market was saturated. But after a lot of research we felt we understood how the key to success lay in our distinctiveness. Our concept was, and is, unique."

To call it unique is not only understatement, but irony as well. Lone Ranger's is a chain consisting of only one restaurant.

"In the early days, nobody understood what we were trying to do," remembers Jack Brattle, sales VP. "People wanted to buy franchises for locations all over the country. But the idea was that there could only be one Lone Ranger's, right?"

Lone Ranger's started in a converted gas station on the outskirts of Lebanon, a location picked because it is generally accepted as the geographic center of the United States. Dunster and his colleagues felt that, sooner or later, the people would come to them. Expansion did occur via franchising, but always in the same location. This meant building self-contained units as annexes to the original restaurant, and today Lone Ranger's covers an area some two miles in diameter. The company incorporated itself as a town last year, and it has its own ZIP code for its more than 2,600 distinct but virtually identical restaurants. These "stores" are connected by a maze of sidewalks, driveways, shared parking lots, and trails, punctuated at regular intervals by huge silver bullet shaped trash cans. Corporate headquarters are in the center, perched atop a twenty story structure erected over the original restaurant.

The Wild West décor is about what one would expect, and the menu can be described as only moderately inspired, although pricing is competitive. Heading the list is the popular Hi-Yo Silverburger at $3.49, a large sandwich consisting of the usual double patties of ground beef, cheese, lettuce, tomato and onion but served on thick slices of patented round Texas toast instead of a sesame seed bun, with a choice of barbecue sauce or ranch dressing and garnished with a sprig of sage. Then there are the Silverfish Filet sandwich at $1.79, bullet-shaped Gringo Fries, and the inevitable Tonto Turnovers for dessert. Drinks include Sasperilly Soda (root beer) in sizes by "caliber" instead of ounces and including the .45 caliber Big Gulch. Masked Milkshakes flavors are randomly selected by spinning the cylinder of a toy six-gun at the ordering counter.

Single patty Kemosabeburgers are popular with smaller appetites (99¢), and a somewhat controversial sandwich of lettuce, tomato and pork rinds known as the "What-You-Mean-Wee-on-White, Man?" looks to hit a bull's-eye with minorities. One innovation being tested in eighteen restaurants is the Butch Caven Dish, a three course combo meal for "gangs" of four or more.

To encourage repeat visits and brand loyalty, Lone Ranger's recently launched a children's club called The Gettem up Scouts.

People do come, in droves, making Lone Ranger's a legendary tourist destination and spawning countless motels, outlet malls, RV parks, and weekend dude ranches off the highways leading from Omaha, Wichita and Kansas City.

But sales have been tumbling since reaching their all-time high two years ago. Profits are beginning to erode like a desert arroyo, leaving a bitter taste in the mouths of many once happy investors. Cynical wags suggest the problem is simply the incessant playing of "The William Tell Overture" in every store, but knowledgeable observers cite too-rapid expansion as the root cause of the company's current dilemma and tend to blame the youthful Dunster for being overenthusiastic in the early days. "Sure, maybe I was kind of a cowboy then," he says, shrugging off the Whiz Kid epithets he is hearing with increasing regularity, "but you have to start somewhere. If we hadn't done it, you bet somebody else would have."

In the eyes of operations VP Brewster Lamont, the speed of the expansion had nothing to do with it. "It was our expansion model itself," he says flatly. "As we continued to surround the inner core with concentric circles of new stores, naturally sales fell off in the center since customers wouldn't bother to penetrate very far except during the peak hours when the outer stores overflowed."

When the ratio of perimeter-to-core units rises, as it must in a concentric growth model, average sales and profits per store drop.

Scores of franchise owners in the decaying central sections have simply abandoned their stores. Hundreds of others are waging a campaign for greater visibility to attract customers. They propose raising their stores several stories up on stilt-like structures so they can be seen from the perimeter. Customers would reach them by elevator or, in some cases, by large ramps. Corporate planners have already commissioned architectural drawings for what in two more years would amount to a hollow teepee of hamburgers 150 feet high.

Development of a theme park on adjacent acreage is under consideration as well, which might bring in even more tourists and spike repeat business for the restaurants.

"We have reservations about these projects because financing is a big problem, particularly in today's economy," admits CFO Radcliffe Bunting. Even so, some on Wall Street argue that with the market now recovering from historical lows the timing is good for an influx of capital through a new issue of stock. Lone Ranger's has turned down opportunities to be listed on the Big Board, reasoning that it just makes more sense, as a fast food restaurant operation, to be traded over the counter.

Outside pressure from the Smith County Sheriff and the Lebanon Town Council is also being felt. There is a crime problem within the 74 million square foot complex. Daylight muggings, and worse, are common. In the past two years six franchise owners whose stores are near the center have been convicted of armed robbery of other, more prosperous, stores. Fourteen more robberies remain unsolved. The abandoned stores have become a campsite for homeless people from all over the Midwest as well as secure hideouts for robbers, some reportedly from as far away as Denver. Partly in response to all this, some of the worst-performing stores are being converted into ranch-style townhouse condos for families of franchisees and employees who prefer not to commute from Lebanon or other nearby towns.

A Community Watch has been organized in the residential section, but each new incident brings it closer to becoming a vigilante group. Corporate security forces are limited and will apparently stay that way as a matter of policy. "But, let's face it," says one frightened perimeter franchisee, "there's only so much one masked man patrolling on horseback can do, even if he does have a faithful Indian companion."

Through it all, founder Dunster refuses to adopt a "circle the wagons" attitude, however mindful of the irony, believing the daring and resourcefulness that carried the company this far will yet bring back the thrilling days of yesteryear. But decisions need to be made about how to spur renewed growth. A freeze on further expansion and a commitment to redevelopment of the blighted areas is one alternative. The theme park is another. If the company must expand, a linear growth model, rather than the historical concentric one, would at least stabilize the critical perimeter/core ratio. And maybe some new music would help.

In any case, at Lone Ranger's it is clearly time to bite the bullet.

Washing Machine Trilogy

(Co-written with Stephanie Thomas)
Inquiring by e-mail of an honest friend
working at an appliance outlet store

Wash

Hi Stephanie,

Since you work at the outlet, we've questions for you.
We need a new washer so what shall we do?
Do you sell really good ones; is your brand the best?
Can you point to the right one and ignore the rest?

We want a top loader that's standard in size.
Three point six cubic feet seems just right to our eyes.
And if inches of width were about twenty-seven
the fit would propel us to laundry room heaven.

The color's no problem, most everything's white
which will match our old dryer whose life is not quite
a study in failure, at least not just yet,
so to keep it a season's a pretty good bet.

Or would it be better to spring for a pair
of matching appliances just to be fair?
Do discounts apply for such a fresh start
or is this kind of thinking not really so smart?

You're having a sale and we're ready to buy
if the quality's great and the price not sky high.
Oh, and do you deliver, install and take care
to dispose of the old one for no added fare?

Rinse

Hi Walt,

We have what you need,
but please do take heed.
The things that I sell
are not always so swell.

It's true, I have learned
that most are returns,
for they have been used,
maybe even abused.

It has been suggested
the washers are tested.
Though I be no sleuth
this is not the truth.

Once they leave my store
there are problems galore,
with fire and smoke,
this is not a joke.

We deliver on trucks
for sixty-five bucks,
take the old one away
for ten more that day.

What I say is true,
I don't want this for you.
If you choose to buy here
I say buyer beware!!!!!

Spin Dry

Hi Stephanie,

Your *caveat emptor* is wise on its face,
and we're grateful to know it will save us disgrace.
Through friends in high places one oft gets a deal,
but here it's the seller who looks for a steal.

You're so very nice with your candid advice.
You've given us pause and made us think twice
about buying from you with the risk so involved.
We'll continue to search till our problem is solved.

If GE is good and new Whirlpools are too
and competitive prices are there to pursue
and if quality ratings result in good scores,
then we'll eschew the outlet for regular stores.

So that's our new plan, to keep looking around
for there must be a bargain somewhere in this town.
We'll search in the paper, watch ads on the telly
and make a good buy 'fore our clothes get too smelly.

Good Humor, Inc., Local Assets Frozen
First in a series of human interest obituaries

From *The Other Village Newspaper*

The local Good Humor Man, known to his friends as Orlando "Caramel Crunch" Toppazini and a respected member of the local business community, died late yesterday afternoon.

The carbon dioxide from the dry ice in his truck's freezer apparently asphyxiated him when he stopped too long to dally with Mrs O'Leary, the Jack & Jill driver. His employers stated he had only one more day to try to unload 100 boxes of their new, pizza-flavored Popsicles before they would cite him for poor salesmanship. Police counted 99 boxes in his truck.

Toppazini died with his hand on the little tin bells which had endeared him to thousands, up until about a month ago when he started trying to sell the new PizzaPops.

Besides his estranged wife, Emma, Toppazini leaves a son, Drumstick, 34, and a daughter, Fudgie, 7. Services will be held in the chapel at the Winters Funeral Home & Frozen Foods Company at 2:00 p.m. Sunday, with Rev. Dr Robert ("Rocky") Rhodes officiating and longtime family friend Humus B Kiddin delivering the eulogy.

Winter Olympics

Snow.
Racing up the hill,
up the little hill to the very top and then
back down.
Fast.
Only one ski, and broken,
so we pass it around,
sharing the challenge.
Flexible Flyers are okay for the little kids,
safe on their tummies, unworthy targets.
Better to dodge the snowballs standing up, on one leg.
Invincible.

Hercules in Dutch

(Published in *Ours: A Poetry Anthology*
from Fantastic Books Publishing)

Hercule Poirot from Brussels sprouts
and plants himself in London
with Captain Hastings as his scout
and capable Miss Lemon.

Detecting crimes and miscreants
across the English map,
athwart benighted salience
the Chief Inspector Japp

By Scotland Yard he's held in awe.
The criminals all rue him.
No plot too thick or threat too raw
can foil him or subdue him.

Perceiving all the subtle clues,
the paragon of minds
His methods and his prey each use
grey cells of different kinds.

But nothing lasts forever here.
In time the best have stumbled.
A web of evidence unclear,
a reputation humbled.

And lo there comes a season black,
the case he cannot fathom.

Hercule prepares his best attack –
Alors, a mental spasm.

Torn with doubt, which thread to follow?
Vacillation awful.
Friends and foes with laughter hollow
see the Belgian waffle

Hot Weather

A modern 60's rockabilly reminiscence.
Think Buddy Holly and Bo Diddley meet the late Steve Jobs.

Hot weather's here and school is out.
What're we gonna do when we're out 'n' about?
Don't want to Twitter my time away;
text my circle, see what they say.

Ought-a get a job to help make ends meet –
Get enough gas to keep my car on the street.
But flippin' Big Macs in a hot fry pan?
Forget about that, I got a better plan.

Run to the river and jump right in.
Goin' skinny dippin' with all o' my friends.
Girls might see us, but that's all right.
They'll run away 'cause it'll give 'em a fright.

No gas in my car,
but I'm gonna go far,
'cause I'm practicing hard
on my Wii guitar …

Now fall's comin' on, the nights are cold,
but we're still hangin' out at the swimmin' hole.
Wasted all summer, but I'm all set:
Never once did I get my iPhone wet!

Hippies Revolting

From *Newsweekly Magazine*

IZKRAP, Tibet, April 19: Some 45 years after abandoning Haight-Ashbury in favor of less touristed dystopias, most of the world's few remaining hippies have retreated to a last stronghold, on the roof of the world, insulated, presumably, from the restrictions of Western civilization. But there is apparently trouble in Paradise. From here in Tibet comes word that the commune of some 1,500-odd love makers is having its problems.

In an interview on Tuesday, Brother "Big Fats" (sometimes also known as "Big Joints" for his generosity) Lawrence Dingle, formerly an apprentice encyclopedia salesman in Altoona, PA, who dropped out at age 30 to become self-proclaimed Roof of the World hippie spokesman, commented on the adversities faced by his vocal minority in self-imposed exile.

Speaking from his combination water bed and hookah in the meat locker at the officers club of an abandoned Royal Tibetan Air Force Base, Dingle summed up the situation in few words: "It's that dumb-ass Abominable Snowman."

Pressed for an explanation, he continued. "I mean his hair is long and matted and filthy. He wears rags or darn near goes naked, and like mooches his meals from us, man, or else eats from the Dumpster. He crashes where he wants and never works, just staggers around with his eyes kind of glazed over, like a wild animal. He's always rank and smelly, and he never bathes, and he's always coming around wanting to make love. With anybody!

"I mean if the guy don't dig our society, man, is no reason for him to make a big hassle at the same time he's still taking handouts from us. He's got to, like, live up to his responsibilities, you know? Like, we can't understand that kinda bag! Peace, man."

In Izkrap today the authorities were holding their piece too, and if there was any concern over mounting tensions in the mountain tent city at the air base, no one was showing it. Speaking for The Establishment, part-time lama Lamar Llewellyn, 42, a retired encyclopedia editor (Escuage to Hypsometer) from Upper Darby, PA, read a prepared statement to reporters: "I mean, why should I give a crap? I've got mine! Peace yourself. *Namaste*, man."

Next Week: Action news photos of the tragic confrontation (if our news team is successful at bringing something to a head here).

The Punx Club

she stood b4 the witebord as students filed n 4 1st day of class good mornng she sed 2 each 1 please take seat then when settled she sed hello my name sarah jones n ill teach this class n modern msgng well learn 2 write w/o punx or caps a skill u need n this age o txtng n twtng n even emails n fb msgs r writtn mor n mor w/ abbreviations acronyms fonetic spllng n few punx or caps miss jones its mrs jones sorry no prob please say yr name n then ask yr question ok mrs jones im valerie fernandez what if we still need 2 know punx 4 4ml writng 4 like resumes n stuff good question n thats why i invitd mr bill fogarty o english dept mr f

"Thanks, Sarah," said Mr Fogarty who had been waiting by the door. "Here at County Community College we recognize that not everyone who enrolls in the Modern Messaging class wants to become e e cummings so …"

"Mr Fogarty?"

"Yes, Mr … uh …"

"Frank Thompson, sir."

"Mr Thompson."

"Who is e e cummings?"

"Ah, thank you, Mr Thompson. Class, does anyone know the answer?"

A voice in the back of the room piped up. "Wasn't he some kind of poetry dude that didn't like to use capital letters?"

"Yes, well 'poetry dude' doesn't quite do him justice, but you're right, he often didn't use capital letters in his poems or his name, and no one really knows why except it went along with his innovative style. But he did use punctuation occasionally. Which brings us back to why I'm here. I wanted to let you know that if you're interested we're forming a Punctuation Club for those who want to learn more about punctuation and capitalization since you'll probably have to keep using them for some purposes, at least for a while. There's no academic credit for being in the club, but it's free to join, and there are no textbooks to buy. However, you do have to sign up, and we'll be using *The Elements of Style* by Strunk and White in case you want to purchase that, but it's optional. We'll meet on Tuesdays right after this class. I imagine the contrast will be interesting, don't you? I'll leave a sign-up sheet on Mrs Jones' desk."

10q bill sed mrs jones when he fnishd r there any qs 4 mr f no ok 10q again bill mr f lft the room now 4 2days assignmnt i thot wed start w/ somethng challengng throwng u all n2 the deep n so 2 speak but later well break it dwn n small pieces 2 analyze r work dont worry about gettng everythng xacly right n this 1st exercise therell b plenty time 2 learn n mprove as the smester goes on so now please get out yr ipads ifones or smartfones or whatever n mr thompson yes maam would u mind helpng me pass out these sheets 10q now mr t passng out copies of the poem jabberwocky not by e e cummngs but by lewis carroll n what i want u 2 do is txt me the hole poem but leave out all the punx n use lower case where c uses caps ok does every1 understnd the assignmnt good lets bgin my # is n the sheet n ill print out yr work after class grade it n give it back 2 u thurs when well discuss it ok feel free 2 leave when ur finished o n dont 4get the signup sheet 4 the punx clb 10q mrs jones sat at desk n 2k out her ifone

And finally ... The Lost Episode?

Eat your heart out, Ancient Mariner

CHAPTER SEVEN
"The Lost Episode"
Rimes with ...

The racing shell bobbed lazily in the calm water as eight of nine sunburned faces regarded the dull orange sunset on the western horizon. Thirty-four days from shore and the supplies were beginning to run out.

"Stroke," mumbled Coleridge, the coxswain and the smallest of the men, but it was finally too much effort to sustain his voice after so many days of saying the same word over and over, and at this last utterance he slumped forward, dead. His head bobbed lazily in unison with the tiny narrow vessel in which he rode. It had been a long race.

Silent seconds became minutes as the exhausted men drooped as if boneless, each in his own little seat, staring with empty, expressionless eyes now at the dead coxswain, then at the fading dull orange sunset on the western horizon.

"I suppose we ought to bury him or something," suggested Scrod, from starboard, losing hold of his oar and watching it float lazily but irretrievably away from its broken oarlock. "Frankly, when I signed up for the crew team I didn't think I'd ever get this sick of it, but I'm starting to get fed up. Fighting for the ole *alma mater* is one thing, but this is the last time I'm rowing in one of these marathons. Look at us—stuck out in the middle of nowhere, only 28 candy bars left, and now the stupid coxswain kicks off. This whole thing was his idea anyway."

"Aw, shut up, Scrod!" said Krumple, the largest of the eight oarsmen, although all were of less than average height and build, like jockeys, with no unnecessary weight to pull during a race. "All you've done is bitch for the past three weeks. It's time we all relax a little and try to figure out where we go from here."

Krumple grimly unwrapped a candy bar. He examined it with deliberation, turning it over and over in his left hand, but quickly so it wouldn't begin to melt. Finally, he broke it in two and carefully put both pieces into his mouth, closing it instantly so no stray crumbs could escape. He chewed slowly. After a moment he spit out four almonds.

At this, the other men recovered from their lethargy. Scrod leaned back and reached for Krumple's almonds, which had landed under his seat. Krumple's fist caught Scrod just behind and a little below the right ear, causing the smaller man to snap back to his place in time to avoid a second blow aimed just above and a little to the left of his nose. The others began to stir, muttering among themselves, until one of them spoke up.

"This has gone on long enough ..."

"Speak up!"

"I said this has gone on long enough!" It was Stern, from the bow. "We're getting irrational, and to start with I want an explanation for Krumple's odd behavior just now. After all," turning to Krumple, "if you spit out your almonds why can't Scrod have any?"

As if to answer, Krumple began, "I'll answer that! I'm majoring in accounting, as you all know, and taking a few economics courses. I thought it might help balance out my no-good athlete bully type image. It hasn't, but nevertheless I've managed to pick up a few principles which I feel will stand me in good stead in situations where the chips are down, such as they are now. One of them is to look out for the future."

With this, Krumple brought forth from the murky depths of his grimy sweatshirt a large plastic bag which he hefted and shook, feeling its weight and caressing it with his gaze. He opened it, reached under his seat for the four still-drying almonds, and put them carefully into the bag. His gaze then fell on the wrapper he had not yet discarded. He snatched it up greedily and licked it clean before tossing it into the water.

"You see, men, contrary to what you might think, the almonds are my favorite part of the candy bar, so I've been saving them until last. Also I've been saving them against the possibility we might find ourselves stranded out here. And now I'm glad I did. I've kept track, and I figure I have about 800 almonds in here, maybe 900 counting the ones I picked up that you guys threw away. Which I can't figure out because who doesn't like almonds?"

Stern started to raise his hand but thought better of it.

"Now when I get hungry I'm going to eat, so you guys just keep your hands off my bag!"

The men began to grumble again, some wondering aloud how Krumple could have been so cunning as to keep up this practice for 34 days without anybody noticing, but they were quickly silenced by the sudden appearance of a gigantic white albatross. The bird hovered over their narrow, diminutive craft, still bobbing in ever darkening ripples.

"I've always wanted one of those to wear around me neck, y' know." It was Bowman, from the stern.

"Shut up, you idiot. It's swooping down on our food trailer!"

In the gathering gloom one could still barely make out the dim outline of a rubber dinghy following the shell at a distance of about 50 feet, attached by a nylon rope which now and then glistened in the light that still remained from the dull orange sunset on the western horizon. At the start of the race the dinghy had carried 2,000 candy bars and 500 gallons of fresh water. Now practically empty, it still held the precious few stores remaining to the weary oarsmen.

The huge, gross bird sat astraddle the dinghy as if threatening to befoul the crew's only sustenance. The men waited in deathly silence lest any sound or motion frighten the creature and cause it to lose control of itself. A visceral reaction now could mean starvation, or at least very unpleasant condiments.

The bird looked curiously first at the men and then at the supplies beneath it.

Scrod fainted, his head striking the side of the shell with a tap that could be heard plainly by all the men and especially the albatross who was, fortunately at least in some respects, downwind.

The tension mounted. The bird shuffled its feet a bit and squinted at the men. It was indeed a pregnant situation and just too much for Krumple whose only thought was of the 27 remaining candy bars with their 108 almonds. Impulsively, he grabbed the nylon rope and gave it three powerful tugs in an effort to dislodge the feathery, hook billed menace. The albatross squinted harder, shrugged twice, grunted loudly, and laid a huge grayish egg that nestled itself among the candy bars. Then the big bird collapsed and lay limp and panting on top of the egg with one webbed foot dangling in the sea. Apparently it had been a tremendous effort.

"We're not out of the woods yet," said Krumple with relief, "but if we play our cards right we'll have something different for dinner tonight."

"Or the bird'll have us if it wakes up," said Stern.

Gingerly, Krumple and the men on either side of him pulled on the nylon rope, bringing the dinghy closer, ever so slowly closer and away from what had been the dull orange sunset on the western horizon. Holding his oar tightly with both hands, Bowman cautiously raised it over his head.

Jolly Songs to Send You on Your Way

Quito!
(The Panama Hat Song)

I took a little journey down to Panama
For to buy a hat made out of Golden straw
But in my plan there was a little flaw
When I went to Panama and tried to buy
A Panama hat

I found a perfect fit in a village store
But the label said the hat was made in Ecuador!
Said to the man, "Hey *por favor, señor,*"
'Cause I didn't know that Ecuador it makes
The Panama hat

Chorus
Now Quito, Quito is where I want to go
Quito, Quito at Latitude Zero
Quito, Quito, that's where it's at
'Cause Ecuador is where they make
The Panama hat

Now Panama is really very warm and nice
There's a big canal and frosty beer on ice
But Ecuador is my advice
Go a little more south and you will find
The Panama hat

So go to Ecuador and it will be all right
They got pretty girls and the sun so bright
Gonna need a hat to face the noon daylight

So it's good that Ecuador is where they make
The Panama hat

Chorus
Now Quito, Quito is where I want to go
Quito, Quito, they take it nice and slow
Quito, Quito, that's where it's at
'Cause Ecuador is where they make
The Panama hat

The Panama hat has style and fame,
And "Ecuador hat" would not sound the same,
So I guess it's okay that they stole the name …

Chorus
From Quito, Quito that's where I want to go
Quito, Quito, they have the sweet mango
Quito, Quito, that's where it's at
'Cause Ecuador is where they make
The Panama hat

Coda
I thought Panama was where they make the hat
But go to the source now you know better than that
'Cause Ecuador is where they make
The Panama hat

You know, Ecuador is where they make
The Panama hat

The Bellyful Whale

In the style of an old Irish drinking song

Come close and I'll tell you a tale
Of a man and a maid and a bellyful whale
And how they danced to a fiddler one night
'Til the whale ate the maid 'though she put up a fight.

The fiddler, he ran, and that left the man
Who tickled the tail 'til the whale made things right.
The maid he spit out from his big water-spout;
Then the fiddler poured ale, and they drank until light.

"Pray, tell me now what did you see
In that bellyful whale of an evening with me?"
"'Twas dark and lonely as ever I've been,
And I never saw Jonah, if that's what you mean."

Whiskey before Breakfast
Traditional Irish reel. Lyrics by the author

Life is hard when there's nothing to do,
When the days are long and the jobs are few.
Play the fiddle and the flute when there's time to kill,
'Cause musicians don't have any marketable skills.

Playin' all night, drinkin' all day,
Lord, I wish there was another way.
Stokin' up your body with beer and gin,
Then you get up early, start it all again.

Chorus
Well it wears me out like a marathon contest.
Up all night and we never get no rest.
Need to start the day with something that's high test.
That's why it's whiskey before breakfast.

Nobody's happy in the old farmyard.
The weather's crappy and the ground is hard.
Play for a pint, play for a 'tater;
Everybody plays somethin' sooner or later.

Midnight comes and we're havin' good fun.
At the all night pub? Aye, that's the one!
While you're still sleepin' like a log,
We're up lookin' around for some hair o' the dog.

Chorus (reprise)

Well it wears me out like a marathon contest.
Up all night and we never get no rest.
Need to start the day with something that's high test.
That's why it's whiskey before breakfast.

Fallen and Can't Get Up

Another in the style of an old Irish drinking song

Come, let me tell you another tale
for beer, wine and true Irish ale.
Your health, may it never fail;
pour me some more lest I say farewell.

Crossed swords with the best of men,
'though I can't remember when.
Hard fighting from glen to glen,
ever returning to drink again.

I would stand if I was able.
Pass the bottle and pass the cup.
Raise the floor up to the table;
I've fallen and can't get up.

Well the ale's done what a blade can't do.
I'm floored after just a few.
Fair maid with your skirt askew,
aye, from down here it's a lovely view.

I would stand if I was able.
Pass the bottle and pass the cup.
Raise the floor up to the table;
I've fallen and can't get up.

The Potato Song
(It's a mouthful)

Chorus
I'd plant me some potatoes if only I'd a hoe.
I'd have a little garden and plant them row by row.
I'd pray for rain and sunshine and hope the buggers grow.
I'm Irish, yes, and I'd do me best, if only I'd a hoe!

Verses (tune of "The Irish Washerwoman")
Oh there's Irish and Russets and Yellows and Fingerlings,
Pink Eyes and Pontiacs, tubers for everything.
Big Golden Wonders and Almonds and Chiloés,
Burbanks and Roosters and Désirées too!

And there's White ones and Blue ones and Murphys and Idahoes,
Jerseys, Atlantics, Clavelas and Congos and
Royals and Kestrels, King Edwards and Fonteneys.
You find a new one, we'll name it for you!

We'll roast 'em and steam 'em and boil 'em in water, and
Mash 'em with gravy or pour on the butter, or
Bake 'em and stuff 'em with bacon and cheese, we'll
Dice 'em or cube 'em and serve up a stew.

Oh there's hash browns and French fries and chips for a dippin' and
Twice baked potatoes or scalloped au gratin, we'll
Serve 'em in casseroles, just as you please.
I'll have potato cakes, *latkes* for you!

(Here launch into a rousing rendition of "Hava Nagila" with a Klezmer band, followed by reprise of Chorus.)

Chorus (reprise)
I'd plant me some potatoes if only I'd a hoe.
I'd have a little garden and plant them row by row.
I'd pray for rain and sunshine and hope the buggers grow.
I'm Irish, yes, and I'd do me best, if only I'd a hoe!

Epilogue

Hi there (your name)! While you've been reading this book, I've been waiting here in the Epilogue for you to finish it and now you have. Congratulations! And thank you! That is, unless you're someone who just likes to read epilogues first — one of those "Life is short; start with dessert" kind of people. For which I don't blame you. However, I'll assume you're not.

So how was it for you? A visit to a theme park like Disney World or Legoland with new amusements on almost every page? Or more of a walk on the far side of the desert surrounded by sheep, mostly dull but for the occasional burning bush or stampeding gazebo? Or maybe a marathon run through a variety of terrain and unpredictable weather until you found yourself in the zone with reader's high instead of hitting the wall, keeping on keeping on until the glorious end?

Or were you a marathon imposter who starts the race but after a few minutes slips away to a Starbucks for a couple of hours, then grabs a taxi that drops you three blocks from the finish line in time for you to rejoin the real runners, huffing and puffing and wearing a triumphant, self-satisfied grin, just as if you had completed the whole thing? Shame on you! Go back right now and read the bits you skipped! How can you expect to have an intelligent discussion with anyone about this book if you don't?

Never mind the naysayers who claim after reading this book it's impossible to have an intelligent discussion about anything ever again.

Regardless, if you enjoyed reading this even half as much as I enjoyed writing it, and if it made you think a little now and then in spite of the atmospheric mayhem, please show your appreciation to the fine folks at Fantastic Books Publishing by going online to their Book Store at fantasticbooksstore.com, perusing their list and buying more of what's on offer. Or show your appreciation to me, your humble Author, by getting several more copies of *On Shallowed Ground* for friends and enemies alike.

Then, be on the lookout for the sequel. I'm going to call it *Margarita Recipes from Around the World*. It will have pictures and everything.

Walt Pilcher

About the Author

Walt Pilcher's parody radio commercials for Mother Murphy's Moldy Meatballs at age 11 foreshadowed a career in marketing from which he retired as a former CEO of several consumer goods companies, including L'eggs`, the pantyhose in the plastic eggs (yes, really) and Kayser-Roth Corporation. He holds a BA from Wesleyan University and an MBA from Stanford University, is a former Regent University board member and currently serves on the board of Global Awakening, an international evangelistic organization.

Walt's writing CV includes the first issue of *Galileo*; *The Worm Runner's Digest*; the *Fire & Chocolate* poetry anthology of Writers' Group of the Triad; *Fresh, Ancient Paths*, and *O Henry* magazines; and the *Fusion* and *Ours* Sci-Fi and poetry anthologies from Fantastic Books. His business leadership book, *The Five-fold Effect: Unlocking Power Leadership for Amazing Results in Your Organization* (WestBow Press) was a First Horizon Award finalist in the 2015 Eric Hoffer Book competition.

"I do think people generally take themselves too seriously," he says, "and I hope this book can help to alleviate their self-imposed misery in some small way. Yes, the sky may be falling, but what can you do? Buy more copies of *On Shallowed Ground*, for a start. Then pray, a lot."

Walt lives in Greensboro, NC (USA), with his wife, Carol, an artist.

Facebook: facebook.com/walt.pilcher
On LinkedIn as Walt Pilcher: linkedin.com